Hud stepped ac
Marilyn's lab. She wai
and lock before she spo...

"Let me remind you, PI Kincaid, all information you learn here is classified. In fact, I found out yesterday the Government has shown a passing interest in my work."

"Our government?"

"Yes, of course."

"Why?"

"I'm not aware of the specifics. But every application I can come up with sounds like Black Ops, or Army Intelligence, or something equally scary."

"That sounds ominous. Maybe you'd better explain to me exactly what you're doing?"

"If I take you into my confidence, you have to promise you won't tell anyone. If they find out I leaked even one iota of this information, I will disappear. And you might too."

"What do you mean by disappear?"

"I'll be transferred to a lab Heaven-knows-where to continue the work until it's completed, or my contract is up. Hard telling what will happen to you."

This gave him pause. She sounded serious. But how could he rationalize being in possession of crucial information without sharing the data with the DPD—or at least with Marco?

"Promise me."

She was taking a leap of faith in trusting him, and the soulful pleading in her eyes made him want to comply. In fact, he wanted to promise her more than to keep his mouth shut. He wanted to promise her sunsets on the front porch and breakfast on the veranda.

Praise for Gini Rifkin and...

UNDERCOVER OUTLAW
~5 Stars Readers' Favorite Award
~5 Stars Long and Short Reviews

TRAPPER'S MOON
~Winner, Reader's Choice Award, *Still Moments Magazine*
~5 Stars from N.N. Light Book Heaven

COWBOYS, CATTLE, AND CUTTHROATS
~Finalist, Colorado Romance Writers' Beverley Award
~4 Stars from NetGalley

A COWBOY'S FATE
~5 Stars from *Still Moments Magazine*
~Winner of Maple Leaf Award, best short story
~5 Stars from NetGalley

SPECIAL DELIVERY
~Five Stars and Publisher's Pick from *Still Moments Magazine*
~5 Stars from Fall Into Reading Reviews

***SOLACE*: Fae Warriors Book 1**
~5 Stars from N.N. Light Book Heaven
~Finalist, Paranormal, Romance Guild Reviewer's Choice Award

***BLISS*: Fae Warriors Book 2**
~5+ stars from N.N. Light Book Heaven

***PORTENCE*: Fae Warriors Book 3**
"Great ending to a spectacular trilogy!"
~5 Stars from N. N. Light Book Heaven

Fatal Recall

by

Gini Rifkin

This is a work of fiction. Names, characters, places, and incidents are either the product of the author's imagination or are used fictitiously, and any resemblance to actual persons living or dead, business establishments, events, or locales, is entirely coincidental.

Fatal Recall

Contact Information: info@thewildrosepress.com

Cover Art by *Kim Mendoza*

The Wild Rose Press, Inc.
PO Box 708
Adams Basin, NY 14410-0708
Visit us at www.thewildrosepress.com

Publishing History
First Edition, 2021
Trade Paperback ISBN 978-1-5092-3722-7
Digital ISBN 978-1-5092-3845-3

Published in the United States of America

Dedication

Dedicated to my friend, Faith.
Thank you to the Wild Rose Press, and the amazing Amanda Barnett.

Chapter One

October, Denver Colorado.

She didn't deserve to die. Why couldn't he take the money and run?

Screaming, she struggled in the dingy alleyway. He slammed one hand against her chest, pinning her in place. Her head snapped back and hit the cold brick wall at her back. His other hand wielded a knife, the blade glimmering in the moonlight.

She'd always loved the moon. Now this symbol of girlish dreams betrayed her, illuminating this hideous moment of terror about to end in her death.

Kicking and striking out with her fists made no difference—he's so strong. He growled at her as if he were a beast. Hatred radiated from his body like heat off a matchhead. He didn't have to kill her—he wanted to.

Heart pounding, her breath escaped in little gasps.

She should have left with the other girls. She should have waited for the night watchman to escort her to her car. She should have done so many things differently. Now it was too late.

His eyes shone bright. He snarled and snapped his teeth as if ready to tear her apart.

The blade arched through the air—searing pain followed. Now the knife hung suspended before her. As if in slow motion, thick red blood drip…drip…dripped from the razor-sharp metal. Each drop like the ticking of a clock stealing away the remaining seconds of her life.

Thoughts of her boyfriend and the future they would never share blurred through her mind. No life together, no children, no anything. This was all there was. And tomorrow the world would go on as if she had never existed.

They were calling. She knew those voices. She was floating away, going beyond the pain.

With her last bit of strength, she angled her head to one side to stare up at the stars. She refused to let the eyes of this madman be the last thing she saw before dying.

****

Fighting her way back to the here and now, Marilyn tore the virtual reality gear from her head. The horror of what she'd experienced had her flinging the equipment aside as if it were radioactive. She didn't flinch when the fragile VR apparatus hit the floor with a resounding crash.

Overcome by nausea, she bolted from the chair, barely reaching the laboratory disposal unit before vomiting up the high-priced lunch eaten two hours before. With a shaking hand, she shoved the stray strands of hair back from her face and into the bun at the nape of her neck.

Her theory had worked.

But should she thank the Lord or pray for forgiveness for stealing the last thoughts of a dying woman? Falling to her knees, she wept. The coldness of the linoleum seeped through her light wool skirt, and she hugged herself against the shivers racking her body.

When another bout of nausea threatened, she shifted around and sat on the floor, her back against the wall. Blotting away the tears with the sleeve of her lab coat, a few deep breaths helped to settle her nerves and stomach.

This is what she'd been hoping for, had struggled and worked so hard to attain. After all these years, her idea had become reality. What a magnificent achievement—what a terrifying triumph. Three minutes of pure horror. Three minutes of visions locked away in the deep recesses of a dead person's brain.

What now?

She glanced around the room as if an answer might be written on the wall.

Her deceased subject had been murdered by a serial killer. Should she notify the police? Doing so would lead to a lot of inconvenient questions. Besides, she'd only seen a quick flash of the killer's eyes and mouth, not his entire face. Still, she had to tell someone.

Warren came to mind. Bad choice. Lately, he seemed overly curious about her project. Being the chief financial officer for the Kingsley Institute, he would be aware of the large sum of money allocated to her research—a decision not done frivolously.

Involving Warren would complicate matters as well.

She stared at the disposal unit. Today, trying to impress her, he'd taken her to lunch at *Lafontaine's*, the most expensive restaurant in Denver. He'd be aghast to learn the high-priced food and wine was fermenting in a hazardous waste bin.

One thing for sure, she couldn't blurt out her news indiscriminately. Secrecy from other research labs was supremely important. The realm of science, whether for humanitarian needs or for profit, was a dog-eat-dog arrangement—only the alpha animal kept getting the golden cookies in the form of funding.

There was nobody with whom she could celebrate her long-awaited achievement. A rare bit of self-pity tainted her mood. But being alone, and burying herself in her work, had been her idea leaving no one to blame but herself.

A high-pitched alarm severed the quiet. The grating sound shattered her introspection and nearly sent her jumping out of her skin. All Kingsley employees had key cards, which meant an outsider had been buzzed through to the research wing.

Levering up off the floor, Marilyn struggled to her feet. The room spun at a cockeyed angle. Grasping the edge of the stainless-steel counter, she held tight until the dizziness passed.

Now the signal on the door of her personal lab erupted. The shrill bleat sent a shock wave of surprise and concern racing through her. Surely there was some mistake. Nobody ever came to visit her at Kingsley, and her boss hadn't alerted her of any impending meetings.

Walking slowly so as not to jostle her aching head, Marilyn stepped to the door, opened the security panel, and peered out. A human cliché awaited. Tall, dark, and handsome appropriately described the man on the other side. His light green eyes boldly returned her stare.

"Miss Monrose?" He directed the question through the speaker panel.

"Yes."

"I'm Private Investigator Hudson Kincaid. I'd like to ask you a couple of questions." He held up a license encased in black leather.

Not a real cop—was she obligated to speak to him?

The urge to run streaked through her, but there was nowhere to go, and technically she had done nothing wrong—other than not reporting the terrifying results of her research experiment. But how could he have found out about her subjects, or in what manner she obtained her data?

"What do you want? I'm terribly busy today." Maybe she could reschedule, have him come back when she was able to reason logically.

"Like I said. Just a few questions, ma'am."

She ground her teeth at being ma'amed—the word made her feel ancient. "About what?"

"May I come inside?"

She'd rather keep the advantage of the five-inch-thick steel reinforced door between them. "It's a hazardous bio area." Would that scare him off?

He stepped closer and scowled. "Yeah, well so's a good portion of the rest of the world. Open up."

Catching sight of several colleagues gathered farther back in the hallway, she gave in to his request. No use putting on a show for the other *inmates*.

She keyed in the security code, and the door swooshed open breaking the seal. Three fans in the ceiling ramped up to high speed, recycling the room air at a faster rate to offset the security breach.

"Thank you." Without hesitation, the man strode across the threshold. The door at his back closed with an impressive thud, and the lock reset with a loud click.

Marilyn sized him up. She figured he must be close to six-foot-three. Being on the taller side herself, she appreciated and was attracted to men of a decent height.

Conversely, looking up at a person was unusual for her, adding to her growing dislike for this man and his invasion of her privacy.

Standing at ease, he scrutinized the room. Despite his casual manner, she had no doubt behind those engaging eyes his mind registered every detail about her and the laboratory. Now his gaze drifted lazily over the entire length of her body, stopping one degree short of being rude.

She tried not to fidget. Why didn't he speak? He'd said he'd come to ask her questions. "Well?" she prompted, breaking the strained silence. He stared back and forth between her and the name scrawled on his note pad, and his reason for contemplation sank in.

Her name, Marilyn Monrose, spelled so closely to her idol's, often inspired presuppositions as to her appearance, imaginings she couldn't live up to. "Sorry, no blonde hair or luscious curves. I do have a PhD in biochemistry with a minor in quantum technology and neuropsychology. Oh, and I definitely agree diamonds are a girl's best friend."

The man cleared his throat, stifled a grin, and had the decency to restrict his concentration to her face. "I'm investigating a recent spate of murders, Miss Monrose."

"Dr. Monrose."

"Yes, of course. Sorry. Dr. Monrose, I'm sure you've read about them in the newspaper."

Getting down to business, the spark of amusement in his eyes turned dead serious.

This had been a mistake. She shouldn't have let him in. "Who hired you? Who are you working for?"

"Why is that important?"

"I handle classified information."

"You mean for the government?"

"Not exactly, it's classified because of the threat of corporate espionage."

"You're not doing a particularly good job of keeping things quiet. According to the paperwork I've seen, your name is listed on the logbooks at Bancroft labs for each of the victim autopsies. A point of interest, wouldn't you say?"

Balling her hands into fists, she slipped them into the pockets of her lab coat. She hadn't thought those records would be so easily accessed. Her pulse pounded in her temples causing her head to ache all the more. "My presence at the morgue is not unheard of." She worked at sounding nonchalant but didn't think she'd been successful. "I'm employed by the Kingsley Institute, and Kingsley owns Bancroft Labs where the procedures and tests were performed. As a courtesy for the common cause, we often help out by assisting with work from several different law enforcement agencies and hospitals."

"Yes, so I've learned. But Bancroft usually comes into play when there is an overload elsewhere. The city morgue and the Denver Police Department lab were both fully staffed, and business was slow on the nights of the murders."

"I don't know what to tell you. Folks around here do what they're told, no questions asked. Me included."

"And who do you suppose told the chief medical examiner to perform the work at Bancroft rather than at the city morgue?"

"I have no idea who specifically sent out the request." This admission was one step removed from a bald-face lie. To facilitate her research, she had petitioned for the autopsies to be done at Bancroft, but she truly had no idea who made the call. “Was there a problem with my work?” How many of her reports had he managed to track down?

“I’m not here to judge the worth of your expertise. I’m making basic inquiries, following up on a hunch.”

“I’m not sure I like being considered a hunch in a murder investigation.”

He flipped his notepad shut, and along with his pen, he shoved both into the pocket of his sport coat. “It beats being a victim.” There was an unmistakable sincerity in his voice, and he stood taller as if he’d come to personally champion the ignoble deaths of all three women.

As he studied the room, she studied him.

Ruggedly handsome, his sensuous mouth softened the strong cut of his jaw, and the beginnings of a five o’clock shadow highlighted his cheek bones. Midnight brown hair curled down over his collar, a bit too long, and a bit too intriguing.

“What exactly are you working on in here?”

Following one of her VR sessions, the room always seemed in disarray. Had he noticed the pieces of her equipment scattered across the room, or her notes, now an untidy heap on the floor beside her chair. “My theory is rather hard to explain, and right now I’m not at liberty to divulge the details of my project.”

“Can’t or won’t?”

“Both.” Chin up, she squared her shoulders and crossed her arms over her chest. When faced with an obstinate male, she took what she considered her Wonder Woman pose. She wasn’t about to budge on this and wouldn't be intimidated. Gender equality had been slow in reaching the scientific community, and she'd been crossing swords with males and their attitudes since day one. He wouldn't win.

As if in frustration, PI Kincaid ran his left hand through his hair. Clean yet far from manicured, his hands appeared strong and accustomed to work not found behind a desk. He wasn't wearing a wedding band.

As they stood sizing up one another, her gaze slid lower. His white dress shirt was open at the neck, his tie hanging loose and a bit askew as if he'd already had a long day. Straight-legged dark trousers covered the tops of the cowboy boots he wore, and she'd bet there was a Stetson on the front seat of his car—or more likely his truck, parked in the lot.

A haunting weariness overtook his demeanor before he turned and strode toward the door. Did he also have visions he'd like to erase? "Thank you for your time, Dr. Monrose."

Was that all he wanted? Wasn't he going to ask her anything else? She should be glad he was leaving, yet disappointment riffled through her, which made no sense at all. "Wait."

He halted and pivoted to face her, expectation now enlivening his appearance.

"I…I have to key in the code before you can open the door." She hurried across the room.

He stepped to one side yet remained near, and the closeness of his body gave her a little thrill. He smelled clean and earthy. Oh man, bayberry soap.

An image skipped through her mind of him soaking in a clawfoot tub, the room drenched in the soft glow of a kerosene lamp. With a shake of her head the daydream dissolved away, and she keyed in the security numbers. Her experiments were overloading her brain cells again.

The code box clicked, and the green light went on.

Standing at her back, he reached around her. They both grabbed for the doorhandle at the same time and, hands overlapping, they pulled the door open in unison. With one arm, he continued encircling her from behind, and a streak of sensuous pleasure blazed a path from her belly to the crotch of her new Victoria Secret panties.

Oh, for Heaven's sake. She was a well-educated, thirty-year-old woman. She shouldn't act all gangly and intimidated because a handsome cowboy private investigator captivated her with a pensive gaze in those gorgeous green eyes—sad, sincere eyes.

"Thanks again." He slipped around her and ambled out the door and down the hallway. The image projected by his tall, broad-shouldered form left her feeling fine-boned, almost dainty—a sensation she hadn't experienced since before the seventh grade, the year she'd shot up four inches in height and towered over all the boys in her class.

When he disappeared around a corner, she exhaled long and slowly, ordering her senses to simmer down. With the security door closed and the red light on, she felt less vulnerable as she retreated back into the lab.

The trauma and suffering she'd witnessed during the VR experiment seemed to hang in the air, awaiting the return of her undivided attention. Hands gripping the metal countertop, she held on tight as the immensity of what she'd achieved, and what she'd seen, flooded back in full force. Then hot fear of another kind replaced all other sensations.

Right there, inches away and in plain sight, sat a rolled-up EEG strip and a manila envelope labeled *Becky Chapman*. The detective must have seen the printout, yet he hadn't challenged her to hand it over. Did he have the authority to come back with a warrant. Would he share his findings with the Denver PD?

Panic sent her into action. Her experiments related to the murder victims were no longer a secret. She'd better take all her files and computer flash drives home tonight and do whatever necessary to keep this information safe. She couldn't trust anyone—not the police, this private detective, or her boss.

A good bit of Marilyn's work could be done at home. She could catalog the new data and crosscheck the figures. Or review her reactions from this time in comparison to the previous sessions. And there were the side effects to be dealt with—or endured. Also best taken care of at home.

Grabbing a box of newly delivered lab supplies, she emptied the original contents and started jamming everything related to her research into the container. As camouflage, she placed her bedraggled Maidenhair fern on top. Although good at gardening, she had wretched luck with house plants.

Coiling the EEG strip, she gently tucked the old-style, priceless information away with the other items. All her data was computerized, but studying the results hands-on created a personal connection which sometimes sparked intuition.

Becky Chapman, the latest victim, had been killed two days ago…that poor young woman. The fatal recollections Marilyn had viewed returned with a vengeance, bombarding her mentally and physically. The nausea also reappeared, nearly sending her back to the disposal unit.

She stumbled over to the recliner chair and collapsed on the seat, the only soft item in her steel and glass sterile laboratory space. Covering her face with her hands, unstoppable tears began to flow. Against all odds, miraculous and terrifying, she had felt Becky die.

Chapter Two

"Yo, cowboy, that your horse out front?"

Hud Kincaid smiled at the familiar voice with the unmistakable Brooklyn accent. Having taken the liberty of sitting at his ex-partner's desk, he now rose to meet his friend, Marco Moretti.

Wearing plain clothes, the man wended his way across the Denver Police Department squad room. When he drew near, Hud reached for the proffered hand. "Hey detective, how goes it working with the boys in Undercover?"

"The same as when you and I were beat cops in homicide—underpaid and overworked." His buddy dragged him closer for a rough man-hug then stepped back. "The redeeming factor being I usually don't have to wear a suit or a uniform." Marco flicked a finger at Hud's tie. "Looks like that thing tried to strangle you and lost."

"It was a close call. Today I won."

Being a PI often called for tactical situations, requiring clothing ranging from combat gear to civvies, the type of dress conducive to quick action. But for interview purposes, Hud tried to up his game, if not with a full-blown suit, at least with a good pair of slacks and a decent sports jacket. Coaxing the local citizenry to cooperate was hard enough without resembling a down-on-his-luck Sam Spade caricature. But he could hardly wait to get home and into a T-shirt and Levi's.

Marco eased down onto the corner of his desk. "Anything new regarding the case?"

"Nothing helpful." His chat with Dr. Marilyn Monrose hadn't revealed anything concrete—other than the fact she was hiding something. "You?"

"Same here."

Having gotten the go ahead from his old boss at the DPD to share information on the case, Hud met with Marco every few days to touch base and exchange data. Unfortunately, it had been slim pickings lately for the both of them.

"I want this one really bad, Marco."

"We all do, Hud."

His stomach knotted as the morgue photos reared up in the back of his mind. Their most recent victim—Becky Chapman—had been only nineteen years old. Just a kid. "She worked at a bakery at night and went to dancing school during the day. She was going to be a ballerina. Who would friggin' do that to such a little butterfly of a girl?"

"I don't know. It's hard to even imagine. A big chunk of this world sucks, and we've got a ringside seat. But there's still good out there. You gotta dig deeper for it these days. We'll get this maniac."

"Or die trying."

"Your go for broke attitude is showing," Marco warned. "You know that's dangerous."

"Yeah, well that's how I feel right now, dangerous."

"So, get over it. Dead PI's and dead cops don't help anyone."

"Okay, okay. I get the point."

"I hope so." Marco eased upright off the desk. "You need a good dose of R & R. Found a willing woman yet?"

Hud shook his head. To Marco, a woman was the answer to most any problem. Big, small, short, tall, he loved them all. Any time, any place. And with his old-school Italian charm and his new-school bad boy appeal, the majority seemed to love Marco too.

"Take my advice, man, and get back out there. Your breakup with Jennifer was a dirty deal and hit you hard, but it's been a while. Hanging out alone up north on the lone prairie, you'll end up as crazy as the psycho we're chasing."

"Yeah, I hear you."

"And don't start taking the job personally."

Too late. His job was his life. What could be more personal? His work had become the bane of his existence, and ironically the main thing keeping him sane. "I'm all right." Hud knew Marco would see right through the lie. "But I could use a good night's sleep."

"Then go home and get one, cowboy. Even John Wayne slept on occasion."

Marco snagged his leather bomber jacket off the back of the desk chair. "My night, however, is about to get rolling. I'm on second shift, and I need to head out."

"Exactly what are you undercover as?

"Your average Joe in a bar seeking a little professional action."

"They'll never believe you have to pay for it."

"I know, right. The idea does stretch the imagination, but here's hoping they do. We aren't after the women. We're trying to take down the scumbag who pimps them out—and beats them to a pulp if they try to leave his employ or they don't bring in enough cash."

"That sounds like a job for Vice.

"One of his girls ended up dead."

"That's a different story then. Any connection to the other murders?"

"Doubtful. Totally different MO. Probably a one-off. We're fairly sure this guy is guilty, but we can't make it stick. And he alibied out for the time of the other three murders. Was in Vegas during two of them. There's a lot of underground gambling going on around here lately, overseen by a group of nasty characters. We think our pimp might be involved, and that's why he was in Nevada."

Marco checked his Glock 22, the same weapon Hud and most law enforcement personnel carried. Tucking the gun away in the holster at the small of his back, he grabbed a spare magazine holding twenty-two .40 caliber bullets. Shoving the extra ammunition in his jacket pocket, he gave Hud a nod goodbye. "Gotta go, the ladies await."

"They're in for a real treat."

"You got that right. Keep in touch."

After his friend left, Hud studied the precinct room and other officers. There was a time he called the DPD home too. Back then, Marco and he were friends and partners. They were still friends, but the partnership was once removed. No longer working for the same agency, there was the faint odor of competition drifting in the air. They kept the rivalry amicable. The end result, they took dead serious. To them, that's what really mattered.

The higher-ups at the DPD viewed the rivalry with

more zeal. They didn't like the idea of an outsider showing-up the department, and normally Hud wouldn't be allowed to participate. But serial killers on the loose were bad for tourism and re-election. The Governor and Mayor must be breathing down the captain's neck to wrap this up pronto. The man would need all the help he could get.

Hud's gaze drifted over to the Becky Chapman file lying on the desk. No need to open Marco's folder. The info mirrored his, and he knew every word and photo by heart having studied the data into the wee small hours of last night. Did the Chapman file he'd spotted in Dr. Monrose's lab contain anything different? He'd been itching to find out but knew asking would have been pointless.

They had such few facts to go on. Anything new might help. All the victims were brunettes of various ages, working the second shift at jobs requiring them to wear a white smock-like coat. Nothing else seemed to connect the victims. No forensic evidence, no witnesses, no one ever heard or saw anything. Although not altering the end result, there was one positive factor—there had been no indication of sexual assault.

The police had interviewed and investigated each set of family and friends. No links were found between any of them. He tried not to think about the one horrifying detail being kept under-wraps. Surprisingly, no one had leaked this freaky element to the press.

The individual committing these homicides had to be crazy. No sane person could live with himself after committing such murders. But then again, a woman could be responsible, although theories pointed to the perpetrator being a man. Significant force would be needed to wield the attacker's weapon, suspected to be a large military type of knife. Man or woman, the person would be covered in blood. Yet so far, they'd gone unnoticed.

Was the killer clever, or lucky? Hud was counting on the latter, because eventually good fortune ran out, and when the tide turned for this monster, he'd be there waiting—no matter how long it took. Patience was a big part of hunting—whether for an animal or a man. But what bothered him the most was the carnage this madman could wreak while they searched for him.

Deep in thought, he made his way to the parking lot. Marco's joking remark about finding a woman trailed in his wake, which brought Marilyn Monrose to mind. The good doctor had turned out to be interesting in more ways than one—a tall drink of water, and from what he could tell all legs, exactly the way he liked a woman. Even with her hair tamed back into a bun, she was a looker.

Unfortunately, beauty and brains could be a dangerous combination, as exemplified by his ex-girlfriend, Jennifer. The face of a goddess, hiding the personality of a coldhearted vengeful harpy. She'd had plenty of brainpower, at least where computers were concerned, a skill she freely and deviously applied to digging up dirt to further her career.

Jenn fancied herself a High Society reporter for an e-zine gossip rag called The LoDown in LoDo. And she'd do anything for a story. Anything. Which is where hacking into people's personal files came in handy.

Jennifer hated his job as a PI, more for the low pay then any concerns for his safety in a potentially dangerous profession. Due to his skulking around the underbelly of humanity, his social standing was nearly nonexistent and therefore an embarrassment to her.

Remarkably high maintenance, Jennifer wanted more—of everything. Not greed exactly, she seemed to have a missing element in her make-up, some void needing to be filled. He didn't fit neatly into that space.

Would she have stayed if she'd found out about his recent inheritance? Possibly, but what good would that have done? The undeniably satisfying sex had kept them together for a while, but in the end, they'd had nothing else in common.

Besides, there were nights when a man sought a closeness of a different kind. A companionship from a woman he knew would always be there. A woman who didn't need to be constantly impressed in or out of bed. A woman who didn't mind trading in the downtown Denver skyline for a peaceful prairie sunset.

Was Dr. Monrose a city kitty or a country kitten? He pictured her in a low-cut red evening gown, then jeans and a calico blouse. Both images were tantalizing.

Either way, she was up to something. Reaching his truck, he climbed in and slammed the door shut. She'd been nervous when he'd questioned her, and then there'd been the EEG strip and folder in her lab. Any evidence pertaining to Becky Chapman, including medical data, should have been recorded and locked away at police headquarters. He'd dug through and studied everything available, and nowhere was there mention of an EEG procedure having been done except on the logbook at Bancroft Labs.

Maybe the missing reports were an oversight or they had recently come in. He unearthed his smart phone, keyed in the main number for the building behind him. When he got a connection, he entered an extension code for the Denver PD lab.

"Forensics evidence room," the voice of an elderly woman droned.

"Martha, this is Hudson Kincaid."

"Oh, hi, darlin'." Her tone brightened. "How are you these days? I miss seeing you around here."

Hud pictured the widowed lab supervisor patting her gray chignon into place the way she did when he spoke to her in person. "I'm fine. And there're days I miss being there. If you've got a minute, I need a favor."

"Sure, pet, anything for you."

"Check the file and tell me what specimens or test results ordered on the Becky Chapman case remain outstanding."

"Hang on." She put him on hold. He heard a click as she came back on the line. "They're all here except the tox screen and final forensics on the wound."

"Did they run an EEG?"

"No, of course not."

"Are you sure?"

"Look, sweetheart, I don't tell you how to clean your pistol, and you don't tell me how to organize my lab. If I say they didn't, then they didn't."

"All right, all right." He chuckled at her indignation. "Thanks, I owe you one."

"You owe me several. And if you were older and I were younger, we'd meet in the middle and I'd force you to pay up."

"Anytime, Martha, anytime."

"Oh, bull taco, but I love you for saying so. Have a

good evening, Hudson." The line went dead.

He sat for a moment staring out the windshield. Dr. Monrose was in possession of test results not registered on the log or awaiting results. Had she done the same on the other victims? He needed proof besides her sign-in signature at the Bancroft lab. He'd need to search her records. Marco could get permission, but Hud wasn't quite ready to go there.

Why the heck would anyone run an EEG on a dead person? He supposed since the autopsies were sanctioned by the next of kin, she wasn't breaking the law by doing so. But her actions raised several mighty peculiar questions. Apparently, she had an agenda of her own.

Glancing down at his phone, he checked for messages. Dang, there was one from Captain Bradshaw. When Hud worked at the DPD, the man now running the homicide unit had been his lieutenant. They had a difficult history. Not seeing eye to eye on their final case had been the fault of each of them. Resigning had been all Hud's idea.

The time stamp on the call was recent. The phone had been on vibrate, and he hadn't felt it. Figuring the captain was probably still around, Hud got out of his truck and returned to the brick building. Might as well get this over with before he drove home for the night.

Maybe his old boss had new information. Or maybe Bradshaw wanted to rattle Hud's cage and razz him again for quitting the force and going out on his own. Regardless, if he put off the meeting until tomorrow, the reason why would be one more thing to keep him awake tonight.

****

Hud rapped on the glass panel of the open office door. Then without waiting for an invitation, he moseyed into the room. Captain Bradshaw glanced up, shooting him a look not meant to ease the kink between Hud's shoulder blades.

"Close the door." The older man's tone held irritation and fatigue.

Hair graying more of late, his ex-boss had put on a few pounds from sitting behind a desk. In a rare moment of comradery, the captain had divulged that while the promotion had come with honors and better pay, there was the appearance of being put on the shelf. And if not for the damaging bullet wound to the shoulder, the man would be out on the street in the thick of things more often. Hud would always carry his share of guilt for the incident and twist of fate.

"Have a seat." Not minding the older man's grumpy tone, Hud closed the door as requested, dropped onto a chair, and continued watching the paper shuffling.

The captain's injury had occurred when Hud bent the rules to save a kidnapped child. At the time, Hud knew he might have to sacrifice himself to save the kid, and the decision had been solely his own. He hadn't asked for help. The captain, then his lieutenant, had also made his own decision, taking a bullet to save Hud. When Hud had been suspended for not following orders, he'd decided to strike out on his own.

What they'd lived through hadn't diminished Hud's admiration for Bradshaw. His ex-boss was a by-the-book kind of man, professionally and personally, with little regard for whose toes he might step on to get the job done right. This honorable trait often led to the dismay of the Mayor's and Governor's office, and the local press. Despite the way things had turned out, the Captain was one of the best cops Hudson had worked with or for.

"What's new?" The older man finally spoke, adding a familiar gnarly glare—one capable of cracking a suspect being grilled.

Obviously referring to the serial killer case, rather than offering pleasantries, Hud didn't mince words either. "Nothing." Wait for it.

"Why not?"

There we go…why not. Like he hadn't been working hard enough. This case haunted him night and day. He'd wracked his brain and pounded the pavement for weeks, but to no avail. As investigations went, this was the toughest one he'd ever worked.

"All this psycho leaves behind are dead women. No useful clues and nothing to connect him to the victims, or the victims to one another."

The Captain leaned back in his chair, but he appeared anything but relaxed. A layer of dust clung to the state-of-the-art computer sitting on the desk between them. "Assuming the perpetrator is a he, and there seems little doubt, we need to get this guy off the streets. The press is sticking to the story like gum on a shoe."

Nice one. The Captain's rancor regarding Hud becoming a PI was bubbling close to the surface tonight. Still, quitting the force had been the sensible thing to do.

"The mayor and governor are both demanding results. Mostly because both are running for re-election. How this plays out will affect them come voting day."

"I understand, sir. But I can't manufacture evidence where there is none.

"Hudson, you're working with the DPD because you're good and because we need all the help we can get, regardless from what quarter. But my budget is running low for hiring outside personnel. So, kick things up a notch if you want to stay on the payroll."

"Then I guess asking for a few bucks to inspire the snitches would be out of the question. Sweetening the pot would sure help. So far there's no word on the street, just the smell of fear."

"Sorry, no can do. Every employee in every department has their eyes peeled and their nose to the wind on the alert for anything remotely suspicious in relation to the murders. With all the overtime, every department head is stretched to the limit man-wise and financially."

His ex-boss smacked one hand against the side of the computer screen on his desk. The machine gave a squawk as if in surprise, and a ribbon of dust spewed off the far edge. Technology had never been the captain's strong suit. "With all this knowhow available, you'd think we could come up with a lead."

"By chance or concerted effort, the killer has managed to pick territory without CCTV coverage."

"Always the way." The captain shook his head as if in frustration. "We'll catch a break sooner or later. All we can do is stay the course. You know the drill."

****

Hud left the office in a restless mood. Rather than drive directly home, he detoured over to the Cheeseman Park area of Denver.

Being an old established part of town, the brick

streets were lined with towering trees, and the quiet stately atmosphere warned visitors to mind their manners. The types of residences ranged from turn of the century four-squares to ultra-modern townhomes and condos. Although the park was reputed to be haunted, the closer you got to the green space and trees, the more the home prices soared.

Easing to a stop across from Dr. Monrose's Victorian abode, he cut the engine, tilted back the driver's seat, and settled in. The lawn was tended—hired or the personal touch? The house needed repair, with bits of work obviously in progress. He was happy she didn't live in a sterile high-rise. A BMW Z4 sat outside. This made him less happy.

According to the DMV Marilyn drove a restored VW bug—bright yellow with a ragtop.

He pictured the car and the lady of the house. What had growing up with a name like Marilyn Monrose been like? I mean come on. The spelling was so darn close, conjuring everything this Marilyn was not. Did she find the circumstances amusing, or had her name warped her personality since childhood?

Of course, with a name like Hudson, he had little room to talk. Depending on your age and from where you hailed, his own moniker might conjure visions of a river, a classic car, or a small town on the plains east of Denver.

Using the DPD app on his phone, he ran the plates on the BMW. Warren Jameson's name came up. The car was leased, not owned. Jameson liked nice things. The man worked for the Kingsley Institute, in the finance department. No priors other than traffic stops for speeding around in his snazzy little car. Could this be an office romance?

As the sun dipped lower, lights on the outside of Dr. Monrose's house flickered on, and two now glowed inside. Hud wished he were at home. Nothing beat watching a fiery sunset fade to black behind the Rocky Mountains—sitting by the barn, a beer in one hand, his dogs at his side, the sound of his animals happily munching away on their evening allotment of hay. The perfect ending to any day, no matter how brutal.

Popping open the glove compartment of the truck, he snagged a protein bar kept for emergencies. He hadn't had a decent meal since breakfast, which sounded like a genuine emergency to his stomach. The snack had seen better days. He picked off the bits of wrapper welded to the caramel parts. Replenishing the stash more often sounded like a good idea.

Chomping down on the stale nuts, oats, and soy bits, he promised to get with the program and start taking better care of himself. If he didn't, he'd burn out before they caught this guy.

Finished gnawing on the quick-fix food, he let out a heavy sigh. Usually, he didn't let a case get under his skin. But this one was wearing him down. Three women with their lives ahead of them, snuffed out before they had a chance to discover all the world had in store for them. And they had been murdered in a grisly manner. While working with the DPD, he'd seen his share of inhumanity and cruelty, but this went beyond the pale. He could hardly wrap his mind around such wanton death and destruction.

Although not opposed to breaking the rules when necessary, Hud believed in an orderly existence. One that made sense, like the coming and going of the seasons. He might not like three feet of snow piled up against the barn door in the winter, or sweating half to death doing chores in 100-degree heat in the summer, but he understood these things, knew they would pass, knew they would be offset by brilliant spring mornings and mind-blowing fall colors. There wasn't anything he could think of to compensate for the kind of madness they were up against now.

Sensing movement, Hud jerked to attention. The cheerful blue front door on Marilyn's house opened, and a man appeared. The DMV photo confirmed the person was Warren Jameson. On the way out, the guy gave Dr. Monrose a peck on the cheek. The door quickly closed at his back, no lingering gazes or cute waves goodbye.

Jameson sauntered down the front steps and slid into the BMW. A moment later, the engine rumbled and the car sped down the street. Although none of his business, he was glad Jameson wasn't staying overnight at Dr. Monrose's. Friday night was made for romance, with breakfast in bed on Saturday morning. Such intimacy didn't seem to be happening here.

He shook his head. Why did he even care? Marco was to blame, putting those relationship notions in his brain. Yet he couldn't deny there'd been a spark of interest triggered during his interview with Dr. Monrose. Slow down, he cautioned. You don't need a woman in your life, especially a woman with secrets related to this case.

One by one the lights went off inside the house.

Hud started his truck and eased away from the curb. Taking the backroads north out of the overcrowded city, he headed for his piece of paradise.

****

Marilyn's thoughts began to wander. She should go to bed. The virtual reality sessions sucked the energy out of her mentally. Physically, the experiments left her wired, as if she'd been exposed to an electrical field. Hence the reason she hadn't cancelled her date with Warren. He was generally a fun distraction, and she knew sleep would be a long way off.

She and Warren had watched a movie, and then done some serious kissing on the couch. She was glad Warren hadn't once again pleaded his case for staying overnight. There were times she longed for a more intimate relationship and a special person in her life, but not Warren with his perfectly trimmed hair and nails, and his fully tanned body covered in designer clothing. A living breathing ad for GQ magazine, he spent more time in front of a mirror than most women she knew. Definitely not the building a relationship type.

His priorities were money and scrambling up the Kingsley Institute ladder—as well as the Denver social ladder. Where she was concerned, he showed a keen interest in her work but in little else. He never noticed the progress she'd made in restoring her big old Victorian house—the type of residence she had always dreamed of owning. And he never offered to help.

So what if the place was a bit of a money-pit? She made good wages, on what else should she spend her earnings? But the cash wouldn't keep coming in if she didn't keep making advancements at work.

Speaking of which… Barefooted, she padded over to the foyer and removed the decoy plant from the box she'd dragged home tonight. The flash drives and paperwork underneath needed to be locked away.

She stopped short, a frown creasing her brow. When she'd come home, she'd set the box beside the hall table, not on the top. How did it get up there? And the EEG strip was unwound, no longer secured by the clip she'd attached to the paper printout.

Checking the briefcase she carried back and forth to work each day, she found the combination lock showed random numbers. She routinely set the dials to all zeros. Maybe she'd forgotten. Not likely. Someone had tried to open the carry-all.

She glanced toward the front door and conjured an image of Warren. They'd been together all night, except when she'd gone to retrieve a second bottle of merlot stored in the corner of the basement affectionately dubbed the wine cellar. Was he spying on her? Maybe the paranoia haranguing her emotions of late came with good reason.

Other neuro labs would love to get their hands on her project. The state-of-the-art information would be worth a fortune on the dark web, and she didn't want to imagine how the process could be used in the wrong hands.

Opening the case and gathering the large pieces of crucial information which would not fit in her tiny bedroom wall safe, she transferred and locked up the data in the big roll top desk in the library—or what would be the library if she ever finished refurbishing and redecorating.

Carrying the smaller items, including the flash drives and EEG strips, she climbed the steps to her bedroom and locked these items away too. Sleep seemed hours away, but fortunately several books awaited her on the bedside stand. She'd read until she drifted off. Of course, sleep meant nightmares. They came with the territory. After experiencing such tragedy in super-virtual reality, not having nightmares would seem odd.

Shedding her clothes, she tossed the items over the back of the chair beside the bed. Then she slipped into an ultra-soft set of PJ top and bottoms, the ones picturing kittens playing with a ball of yarn.

Lately, adult styles seemed to be reverting back to childhood fantasies, and she felt about twelve years old as she fluffed up the pillows and then got cozy under the covers. Eyeing the to-be-read pile, she grabbed the book on top.

Before she'd read two pages, a craving for pizza with everything on it streaked through her. Or maybe a greasy cheeseburger and a basket of fries. Where were these ideas coming from? She rarely indulged in high caloric delights. This wasn't like her at all.

Since she'd hit the big three oh, gaining weight without noticing came easily, so she tried to monitor what she ate. Guilt might be triggering the fast-food urge. Telling lies, or at least not coming clean to PI Hudson Kincaid, had been difficult and against her character as well. His questioning and body language indicated he felt her answers left something to be desired.

His visit left her desiring something too. Something she hadn't felt in long, long time.

Chapter Three

Morning sunlight wormed its way through the cracked window then crawled across the filthy mattress. With a groan, Archie rolled to the far side of the bed. Today, even this tiny brightness hurt his eyes.

Rusted and lopsided, the bedframe squeaked and squawked as he twisted around and sat up in the shadows, his back against the damp basement wall. Deathly quiet, his hiding place felt like being home.

The floors above in the condemned apartment building were slightly more livable, but he deserved to be down here. Isn't that right? He glanced around, waiting for an answer. None came—he must be imagining a different basement and a different time.

His stomach grumbled. He'd gone hungry back then too.

Empty fast-food containers littered the top of his table—a plywood board balanced on an empty oil drum. If he wanted a decent meal this morning, he'd have to panhandle for money. Another dose of humiliation, an emotion that followed him like a belligerent stray animal.

Struggling upright, he sat on the edge of the bed. At the sound of a police car siren on a nearby street, his back went rigid. When the noise faded, he relaxed. They hadn't turned down the dirt alleyway leading to his lair.

He'd chosen the derelict building for the location, adjacent to the Denver Zoo. And the night he'd come home from his last mission, he'd heard one of the big cats roaring. Perhaps a tiger, *Panthera tigris*, the biggest of the felines. The sound had been mighty, as if in congratulations for his successful hunt—but the growl had turned melancholy toward the end.

The beasts in the zoo no longer knew the ecstasy of the kill, if ever they had. Yet, even raised in captivity, the desire to hunt must surely be locked into every cat's DNA.

Closing his eyes, he tried to become one with the tiger. Archie had been caged for many years too. Always being told what to do. Forced to take the pills to make him forget about hunting. All drugged up, a tiger had no choice but to rest and wait. His eyes snapped open. The waiting was over.

When he was a child, he'd had a real cat, his best friend. And they'd given him a cat at the sanitarium. Both were gone—one by the hand of his mother and one by the hand of God—each hand equally cruel and unforgiving.

He shivered at the memories, wishing he had the tiger's gold and black striped fur coat to keep him warm. Then coats of another color came to mind. White coats made of stiff starched cotton. White coats covering black evil ways. She kept trying to fool him by wearing different faces, but he always recognized her—the coat gave her away.

Cats killed to survive. He killed because she wouldn't stay dead.

****

Warren Jameson lowered the car window as he

eased up to the bank's drive-thru kiosk.

Up early today, and having filled out the necessary papers in advance, he placed his withdrawal slip in the pneumatic tube and sent the request on its way. Would ten thousand dollars be enough? Could he double the amount at tonight's poker game? He'd better, if he had any hope of digging himself out of the financial hole into which he'd fallen.

He was behind on his mortgage payment for the loft, as well as with his lease payments on the BMW. He caressed the leather covered steering wheel. He loved driving this car—and in or out of the 382-horsepower beauty, he loved moving in the fast lane.

He'd been naïve imagining he was ready for the big time. Playing with these high rollers had turned out to be harder than anticipated. Now he owed big money to some bad hombres. Denver's asphalt jungle, filled with drug dealers, addicts, and camps of the homeless, was only slightly more dangerous than Denver's elite social jungle.

If he came up empty tonight, he'd be forced to implement one of his more perilous strategies. Or maybe he should save the ten grand and just go straight for his end game.

The pneumatic tube came shushing back jarring his thoughts. He reached for his money, carefully counting the large bills before relinquishing his spot to the next car.

He should give Marilyn a call. As he cruised down the street, he grabbed his cell phone, pulled up her number, and hit enter. No answer. Good. He'd rather leave a message. Good morning, gorgeous. Thank you for an amazing evening. Can't get you out of my mind.

Talk soon. Blah blah blah.

She ought to be thanking him for even bothering with her. She was actually rather reserved and proper, keeping him at bay physically, restricting their time together to watching movies and cuddling on the couch. For some reason, she didn't seem all that into him. Well, there were plenty of women who wanted what he could give them. Unfortunately, right now, Marilyn was the one woman who could give him what he wanted.

Based on the amount of money Kingsley threw in her direction, the project she worked on had to be a big deal. But what? Marilyn had become elusive regarding her research.

A variety of scientists were employed at the institute, their expertise ranging from biological R&D, to aerospace, to neuroscience—Marilyn's specialty. Being the company's financial advisor, he knew who got what and how often. He might need to steal a slice or two of that money pie.

Marilyn. His mind drifted back to last night. She really wasn't his type. He went for women in her near-namesake category—blonde bombshells who turned heads. Marilyn seemed more of a homebody, happy to spend her free time refinishing cupboards or planting gardens. What an unmitigated bore. And lately even those hobbies had fallen by the wayside as she showed a concerted effort—to the point of obsession—for her experiments.

Would she be at the lab today, Saturday morning? More likely working at home. He could swing by this afternoon. Bring her a box of pastries. In the Denver/Boulder area, junk food shaming permeated the air, along with the other social justice warrior nonsense.

And previously, such an offering would have pissed her off. Now, he wasn't exactly sure how she would react to the idea.

Last weekend, he'd managed to drag her to a museum exhibit, after which they'd grabbed dinner and she'd readily torn into a taco platter. Come to think of it, she'd been doing several things out of character lately. Women… On second thought, he didn't want to be around her or anybody today. All he could think about was tonight.

About to pocket his cell phone, it rang.

Damn, it was them. The time for deliberation was over.

A cold sweat threatened to ruin his Louis Vuitton shirt. He had to face the facts. Winning tonight would be a temporary solution to his problem. And losing would buy him a trip to the emergency room—or worse. He had no choice. His answer was obvious.

"I'll do it." He forced the words out before he could change his mind.

"Once I tell them, there's no going back."

"I understand."

The sunlight seemed to grow dimmer.

****

Full of nervous energy, Marilyn circled aimlessly around the first floor of her house, her bare feet making soft slapping sounds on the wood floor she kept meaning to refinish. Hours of paperwork awaited, but this morning she couldn't seem to sit still or concentrate. Yesterday's VR session still had her senses stirred up.

Her phone rang for a second time in the last few minutes. Hopefully not Warren again. She hadn't felt like talking and had let his call go to voice mail. Their relationship held little promise of going anywhere. The spark just wasn't there. She shouldn't keep him hanging on and hanging around. Playing false wasn't her style. But sometimes she was lonely.

At the persistent ringing, she gave in and sprinted down the hall to the library. Retrieving the cell phone off the desk, she checked the incoming name, and her eyebrows shot up. Not Warren. Worse. Jade, her boss.

"Hi Jade. What's up?"

"I need a progress report for your current project—on my desk Monday morning."

"Why the rush? I still have a multitude of tests to run on the theory, and—"

"This came from the top. There are rumblings on the dark web all of a sudden, and I'm getting pressure for this to go public before word leaks out. Or before another corporation claims the same idea. Whether it turns out good or bad, useful or not, it's ours."

"Jade, you can't. It's far from ready. And—"

"Do it or the funding will be cut, and Kingsley will sue you for breach of contract."

"But—" The line went dead.

Marilyn set the phone aside as if it were carved of the finest crystal. Eyes half closed, she cradled her head in her hands and returned to walking, walking, walking. She knew the path through the house by heart—kitchen, dining room, front room, foyer. Over and over the strange litany ran through her brain, blocking out the bad news, distracting her thoughts, keeping her brain from fragmenting into a thousand pieces. Keeping her from reliving the last three minutes of Becky Chapman's life.

Hands at her sides, she wandered into the kitchen and stared at the old-fashioned temperature gauge hanging outside the window by the sink. The early morning chill had worn off. Exercising might help. She needed a good dose of fresh air.

Changing from sweatpants and a fleece pullover to jogging pants, a T-shirt, and a cotton hoodie, she laced up her cross-trainers, grabbed her keys, and raced out the front door and down the steps.

Dry autumn leaves littered the path, crunching underfoot and swirling around her feet. The brilliant blue sky held not one cloud, although the dampness and humidity from last night's sprinkling of rain remained hovering in the air. As she ran, she reached up and tightened the scrunchie holding her ponytail.

The trail she followed meandered through the park, and she picked up speed. Faster, go faster. Forget Jade, forget the job—forget the fear. Her heart pounded, and her lungs felt ready to burst. Maybe she would die—for real.

Having recently fine-tuned her equipment, the latest VR experience had been excruciatingly vivid. The visions, deeply ingrained in her memory banks, twisted and snarled with her own. The mash-up of memories had her feeling as if she'd already died twice, once with each of the last two victims.

Breathing hard, Marilyn jumped across a small puddle.

The mundane action she'd intended transformed into an exaggerated leap culminating in a pirouette. What the heck? Oh my gosh, Becky Chapman the dancer was here. Flashes from the victims' lives sometimes slipped into her world. These moments in time had her questioning what was real regarding her physical urges and her mental status. Desperate for a way to find balance, last night she'd come up with the two-brain strategy.

When unusual and unexpected impulses seized her, she attributed them to the New Brain section of her gray matter—the part carved out by the virtual reality sessions. After isolating the responses, her Old Brain could then more logically sort out the data accepting or ignoring the compulsions. A work in progress, the theory wasn't always successful.

She couldn't help but feel a kinship with these women and, when considering them as a collective group, she held internal conversations with them. So far, there was no evidence to prove the females knew one another, but even Alicia Cartwright, the first victim, seemed to hover near. Marilyn hadn't been able to obtain an EEG from Alicia, but she bet their spirits were all together waiting for justice.

Keeping up her pace, she gasped out the words. "I won't give up. I promise." And she meant every bit of that oath with every fiber of her being. The young women had never been abstract subjects in her experiments.

When Alicia Cartwright had been murdered, the public had prayed her death was a onetime atrocity. Permission for the autopsy to be performed at Bancroft, and for her to be involved, had been a last-minute arrangement.

The M.E., a misogynist who viewed women as being suited for handing off surgical instruments rather than wielding them, had arrived first. Upon learning his space was to be invaded by Marilyn and her experiment, the resentful fool had retaliated by opening Alicia Cartwright's cranium and dissecting her brain before Marilyn had even stepped foot in the morgue. She hadn't bothered setting up her equipment. Still, she mourned Alicia's death too.

Muscles aching, Marilyn wanted to turn around and head for home, but recalling the ME's sabotage gave her a burst of angry energy, propelling her onward.

"Don't stop when you're tired, stop when you're done."

This attempt at encouragement came from the Old Brain, as her idol Marilyn Monroe put in her two cents. The movie star's quotes often popped into Marilyn's head. She called them M & M's—sweet little Marilyn Monroe treats. Usually, they brightened her mood. Today she doubted anything could.

Slowing down to a reasonable pace, she thought about LeAnn Swanson, victim number two. When her body had been found, the fear a serial killer was on the loose pre-empted even the ME's petty concerns. After the higherups at Kingsley read him the riot act, she managed to collect her data uninterrupted. But although the tortured emotions had been vivid, LeAnn's visual virtual reality results had come out blurry.

Marilyn had spent hours fine-tuning the converter, only to learn the young woman had extremely poor eyesight. The woman's glasses had been found smashed to bits at the crime scene. LeAnn Swanson's bad vision caused the distortion, not the equipment.

After missing out on the first procedure and having an anomaly with the second, the flawless replay on Becky, the third victim, had been upsetting to the extreme.

Marilyn had tried pretending the VR session was a random slasher flick—no luck. Unlike sitting before a movie screen, the virtual reality equipment reversed one's focus, forcing the wearer to experience the event from the inside out. No longer a casual observer, she became part of what she saw.

When she felt these women die, a piece of her died too. She had to help find their killer—her killer.

But what about when she ran the EEGs? Was she robbing the dead person of their last spark of vitality, a tiny ember of primeval matter tucked safely away in the far reaches of their brain?

She stole, morphed, and absorbed the matter into her own body. Following a session, she felt energized, an addictive euphoria. But what about them? Had they needed the energy in the great beyond?

Reaching the stone fountain where the trail split, Marilyn slowed to a fast walk and circled the splashing water to head back the way she'd come. A cluster of blue jays scattered into the air, squawking and scolding her for interrupting their drinking and bathing. She shied sideways off the trail.

Swerving back on track, she hurried home. What she'd discovered and was going through weighed heavily on her. Talking to someone, hearing their opinion and perspective, would be a huge help. But the need for secrecy reared up almost as strong. The information mustn't fall into the wrong hands. Or was the Institute already the wrong hands? Jade was becoming more and more demanding. How long could she keep deflecting? Working under these conditions was nerve-wracking.

Of course, her parents championed her endeavors, but her current project leaped beyond their scientific interest. Considering the circumstances and side effects, they would be more concerned about her wellbeing rather than any contribution she made to science or to finding this serial killer.

There had to be somebody she could spill to. Hudson Kincaid came to mind.

Being a big fan of the Magnum PI reruns, she couldn't help being intrigued by meeting a real live private investigator. Add in a hint of cowboy, and she was undeniably attracted. Hold on now. Who was talking, Old Brain or New Brain?

The day Hudson Kincaid had come to scope out her and the lab, she hadn't missed the flash of a holstered weapon beneath his sports coat. He was armed and dangerous, or at least armed and curious—and good looking. Those feelings came from both the Old and New Brain, meaning double trouble and a double dose of he's hot.

At her house, she dragged herself up the front steps as if she'd finished running a marathon. If only she had time for a long soak in her beloved clawfoot tub. Considering today's schedule, an invigorating shower would be a better choice.

This weekend would be over in a flash, and she needed to put together an elusive yet impressive proposal to placate Jade. Would a day and a half be enough time to fabricate a legitimate sounding report?

Chapter Four

Monday morning broke clear and crisp and, heading back to the city on I-25, Hud let his mind wander as he downshifted his truck and crawled along in the usual snarl of traffic.

While enjoying the glorious fall weather, he'd spent the weekend busting butt around the farm as he brooded over the case. When performing mundane tasks, like mucking out stalls and stacking hay, parts of the puzzle often fell into place. Not this time.

There'd been no spark of insight or brilliant revelation. He'd gone over and over the data, trying to find a link between the women. He had to be missing something. There was almost always a connection or something to tie victims together. They'd analyzed the situation inside out, and he craved action.

Late last night, a short list of persons of interest had come through via his home computer. Several were felons who'd served their time. Another group were psych patients, recently released into civilized society—whatever constituted that nowadays. Although the list was not long, the process of elimination guaranteed to be agonizingly slow.

Then there was Dr. Monrose, a lead upon which due diligence needed to be done.

Rather than track her down again at her lab, he decided to invite her to lunch—a prospect fostering mixed emotions. He needed to speak with her, but he wanted to see her in a non-professional manner too and knew he shouldn't.

Exiting the highway, he passed restaurant after restaurant as he neared the inner city. The majority of these were high-end coffee shops and vegetarian/tofu/fusion cafés. He had nothing against weed-eaters or eating healthy—but he had no idea how vegans survived. Each to his own was his policy on most things. But dang it, this was cattle country, and a man shouldn't have to work so hard to find a steakhouse.

He gave thanks once again for his patch of land up north. *His sanctuary.* Homesteaded by Virgil Kincaid, his great-great grandfather, those thirty acres had been passed down from generation to generation. Back in the 1800s, Virgil Kincaid had been a U.S. Marshal, and from all accounts a good one. Apparently, Hud had inherited the law enforcement gene along with the family property and a love for the wide-open spaces.

A few months ago, when Hud's Uncle Louie died, the place should have been willed to Hud's father. But his parents were born, raised, and happily living on the east coast with no interest in the property they called *the wild west*. Hud missed Uncle Lou. They'd shared years of memorable times together hunting and fishing and jawing about everything under the sun.

Moving from or selling the place never entered Hud's mind. Did Dr. Monrose feel the same about her Victorian fixer-upper? Maybe he'd find out at lunch.

He slowed down, changed lanes, and turned a corner, then using the hands-free setup attached to his dashboard, he called Marilyn at her lab. She answered on the sixth ring, irritation floating beneath the surface of her hello.

"Dr. Monrose, this is Hudson Kincaid. Could we meet today for lunch?" Although figuring her for the spinach-wrap kinda gal, he went out on a limb and suggested Rusty's Rib House, a sole survivor from the days when Denver was filled with stock pens and cowboys. "The location's not far from the Institute."

The long pause sent his percentages for success dropping. Then to his surprise, she agreed. "I've never heard of the place, but I'll meet you there. Although I have no idea what more I could possibly tell you regarding your case."

"It's been several days since we found the last victim. If the killer's MO holds true, we're worried he may already be stalking his fourth victim. We really need all the input we can get."

"Of course. I didn't mean to sound uncooperative. Is one o'clock all right? I have a meeting scheduled with my boss which might take a while."

"Sounds great. See you then."

He was lucky Dr. Monrose had agreed to meet with him. She wasn't under any obligation to do so. And at this point, her connection to the case was a bit vague, even if her literal and figurative prints were all over the paperwork. Of course, there was his ulterior motive—he wanted to see her again

****

Putting to good use the time between now and his meet-up with Dr. Monrose, Hud revisited all three murder sites. The high winds and quick deluge of rain over the weekend may have revealed a clue.

Following the order in which the deaths had

occurred, he prowled around each crime scene making sure not to disturb the yellow police tape still cordoning off the areas. The first two locations offered nothing new, but the place where Becky Chapman breathed her last paid off.

A Russian Olive tree partially blocked the entrance to the alley where she died. Those limbs carried nasty thorns over an inch long. In addition to the obvious wounds, Becky's body showed random scratches. Forensics found minute traces of blood on the prickly tree spines indicating when the murderer dragged her into the passageway, her body brushed against the spikey protrusions.

Searching along the pathway he found several small dead branches newly-blown crossways by last night's storm and wind. He also found a shred of plastic, clean except for a spot resembling blue paint. The flexible material clung tenuously to the underbrush, and easing an evidence bag from his shirt pocket, Hud carefully captured the scrap.

Driving across town, he dropped the evidence off at the DPD forensic department, taking time to say hello to Martha and to talk about how this case had the entire city on edge. Then since Marco was still on second shift, he gave the captain a heads up on what he'd found and, with little time to spare, he hightailed it over to Rusty's.

Even running a little late, Hud managed to get there first, blending right in with the cowboy-hatted western wearing crowd. Grabbing a booth in the back with a view of the front door, he ordered a beer. Before he could savor half the glass of foamy goodness, Marilyn Monrose arrived.

Heads turned in her direction as she stood inside the door and searched the room for him. Lab coat gone, she wore a tight rosy red sweater and a black fitted skirt, all balanced atop those long legs and high heeled shoes. With her hair unbound, he almost didn't recognize her. She certainly appeared more lovely than the snapshot photo he'd included in the file folder he'd put together on her. The photo-op picture showed her winning an award for a neurological paper written about the field of dementia.

He stood. When she caught sight of him, she seemed to relax a bit, and her features softened. Glancing neither left nor right, she made a beeline toward him. She seemed shy about the attention she'd drawn.

After allowing her to choose upon which side of the booth to sit, he slid in across from her and, removing his Stetson, he set his hat crown-side down on the space at his side. "Thank you for coming." Before she could reply, the waitress scurried over to take their order.

"Hi Hud. What can I get ya?"

"I'll take the usual, Cassandra. I'm not sure what the lady would like."

Dr. Monrose perused the menu as if the single sheet of paper held the secret to the big bang theory. "I guess I'll try the combo platter."

Hud's and the waitress' eyebrows shot up in surprise. The combo platter wasn't for beginners.

"When in Rome." Marilyn gave a little shrug of her shoulders.

"And to drink?" Cassandra prompted Marilyn.

"A beer is fine. And water on the side please, ice,

no fruit."

A beer… He liked this woman more with each revelation, a questionable indulgence on so many levels. Although following the huge influx of designer breweries in Colorado, drinking beer wasn't limited to steelworkers, bikers, and cowpokes anymore. Now even the rich folk professed to being connoisseurs of the suds.

Forcing himself to quit free associating, Hud got down to business. "Thank you for meeting with me, Dr. Monrose."

"Why don't you call me Marilyn?"

"Great, thank you." He appreciated the option. Out of her laboratory she appeared a heck of a lot less doctor-like. Still, keeping a modicum of distance sounded prudent. "Miss Marilyn, in reviewing the timelines the police have put together, can you tell me your whereabouts on the night of the three murders? That would be August thirty-first, September sixteenth, and October first."

For a moment she appeared taken aback by the question. "Why would you need such information?"

They didn't, really. The police had no good reason to press for a formal interview with her, but being a civilian, he could—and gut instinct told him to investigate a little deeper. "Like I said before, your name is on the Bancroft ledgers."

"And like I said before, I had every right to help out."

"But we still can't find out who made the original request resulting in your being there."

Her complexion deepened, bringing a glow to her cheeks to match her sweater. She wasn't especially good hiding the truth.

"All right, I asked to assist. And a Kingsley backer called in a favor."

The waitress staggered over with their order, interrupting his intentions of probing further. Now Marilyn's eyebrows rose in surprise as the platter, containing every imaginable type of barbequed meat, slid into place before her.

"Yikes, this could feed a family of four."

"Don't worry, they have big take-home containers."

"Do people eat like this every day?"

"No."

She smiled at his answer and picked up a rib. Then her brow furrowed as if in confusion and she returned the sampling back to her plate. "I don't generally eat meat." After that revelation, she seemed to concentrate on the side dishes of potato salad and green beans.

"So why did you want to get involved in such a horrible series of crimes."

"I had no idea there would be a series of tragic deaths, but attending the postmortems was an essential step for testing my new equipment. And before you ask, at this juncture, I have nothing of assistance to offer."

The sincerity warming her honey-brown eyes, convinced him she told the truth. But such a determination should be made by the authorities, not her. He cut into his T-bone steak. Marco could probably get a warrant forcing her to reveal the nature of her secret experiments.

"Even with a warrant you'll be waiting for months. The Institute will back me, and they have a bucket load of lawyers."

She was one step ahead of him. He gave a chuckle. There went that idea.

"A good portion of the work done there truly is confidential, even top-secret government related. And Kingsley is notorious for their ability to create red tape. They find challenging warrants amusing."

Was she warning him off, or merely stating the truth? Either way she'd confirmed his suspicions, big names and big money were behind the research facility. But since they were trying to catch a serial killer, Kingsley might find their influence had limits.

She sipped at the beer and licked a tiny bit of white froth from her upper lip. What would kissing the foam off her mouth taste like? As if noticing his stare, she cast her glance downward and made a valiant attempt at lessening the ample helping of side dishes. Hud lost the fight to keep his mind from wandering back into dangerous personal territory.

"What do you do in your spare time?" The question seemed to grab her attention with more enthusiasm.

"I'm trying to restore a Victorian house. Although I'm beginning to discover there was a reason the price was so low. I had an inspection done prior to purchase, but I swear the house was holding its breath and putting its best foot forward until the guy left and I signed the papers. Now the place has heaved a big sagging sigh of relief, and the fancy Victorian high-button shoes have come off, leaving a barefoot odyssey of unexpected repairs."

Confused yet intrigued by her flowery speech, he tried to follow her house analogy. He bet she read poetry.

"Like this meal"—she nodded toward the table—"I

may have bitten off more than I can chew. It's my first house, and I had such high hopes."

"I can relate. I'm updating an 1888 homestead up north. Everything costs more and takes longer than I anticipated. If you need help, I'd be glad to give you a hand with the heavy lifting. And I have a truck to haul stuff in or out."

What was he saying? He shouldn't be doing this. He'd shifted from hard-hitting interview questions to a pickup line. Her connection to the murders seemed coincidental, but what if she was more involved than they knew. With any luck she'd turn him down.

"Oh, thank you. I may have to take you up on your generous offer."

In for a penny… "I don't work for free though."

Her expression sobered.

"No big deal—a home cooked meal, or maybe decorating advice at my place."

"I suppose that could be arranged." Her smile returned, a reaction he'd like to see in her more frequently, especially if they actually saw one another again. Which they shouldn't.

She glanced at the old railroad clock on the west wall, but reality struck rather than the chiming of the hour. Her eyes widened. "Wow I've got to get back. Do you have a dog?" She stared at the overabundance of food remaining on her plate."

"I do. Two in fact."

"Would they like this for supper?"

"I'm sure they would. But wolfing down a plateful of meat covered in BBQ sauce would probably make them sick. You're a cat person, right."

"Usually, but lately I've had an increased

fascination for all animals, especially dogs."

A curious statement, but then there was a lot about Dr. Monrose he found intriguing. "If you don't mind, I'll still take the food. I can pace myself slightly better than the dogs."

"Great."

Score… Now he wouldn't have to buy groceries tonight on the way home.

Grabbing her purse, she snagged two bills as if they had been lying on top to facilitate a hasty exit. Gaining her feet, she tossed the ten and the twenty on the table and turned to leave.

Hud seized his hat, jammed the Stetson on his head, and stood too. A jolt of loneliness or an equally rare emotion, streaked through him. "May I call you?"

"Apparently you have my number," she quipped over her shoulder.

She hadn't hesitated in her answer. That was a good sign…right?

****

Marilyn left PI Kincaid to finalize the bill and to wrestle with the details of the doggie-bag situation. As she walked out the door, she did her best to keep to a moderate pace, although the desire to give an uncharacteristically girly squeal of excitement made her want to hurry out of earshot as fast as possible.

When Hudson stood up and donned his cowboy hat, she'd almost gone weak-kneed and had to sit back down. In her circle of friends, nobody wore cowboy hats, or cowboy boots, or Levi's off the rack rather than designer jeans. Yet he couldn't have appeared sexier had he been wearing a Brioni suit.

And he drove a truck, not a fancy sports car. She

found that appealing too.

And what was all this stuff about dogs? She didn't dislike dogs, but he'd pegged her correctly for being a cat person. New Brain interference again. Victim number two, LeAnn Swanson, had been a dog groomer and vet assistant. Marilyn bet she was not a vegetarian.

The idiosyncrasies of the victims kept tiptoeing around in her psyche, which made her wonder if the real her was as bowled over by Hudson Kincaid as her heart rate indicated? She took a moment to consider, and then decided those tingly sensations definitely came from the Old Brain too.

Unlocking her car, she slid behind the wheel and coaxed her VW into action. Dealing with the two-brain theory was complicated and somewhat annoying, still a small price to pay if doing so could stop this madman.

She considered the one clue she'd learned so far. Were the authorities aware the perpetrator was a male? Maybe her data was more important than she knew.

When she left work later today, she had better take home a few more items to be stored in the safe in her bedroom. Having been installed by the prior owner, the safe was the one rare item properly working in the old house. The larger items related to her work would still have to take their chances in her rolltop desk.

On the way home, she'd pick up the autographed twelve by eighteen glossy of Marilyn Monroe she'd dropped off to be matted and framed. Properly hung, the picture would be perfect for concealing the location of the safe.

The artwork depicted Marilyn leaning over a balcony staring out over the city. A quote at the bottom read *We are all of us stars, and we deserve to twinkle.*

She'd always found those words comforting, and soon she could wake up to them every morning.

Another M & M popped into her mind *Dogs never bite me, just humans.* And there went another dog reference. There were definitely too many dearly departed vying for her attention.

Chapter Five

As darkness eased closer, Archie pawed through the pile of discarded jumpsuits, rubber gloves, and shoe protectors. He'd found the lot while dumpster diving behind McCluskie's Auto Repair and Paint Shop. The bloody plastic coveralls used on his last mission were safely on their way to the city dump. He'd stuffed them into the back of the garbage truck servicing the alley one street over. An easy task. People ignored vagrants and the homeless.

Setting tonight's coverings aside, he toyed with the knife he'd shoplifted from the Army surplus store when he'd first reached Denver. The weapon was similar to the one he'd found in the trunk in the basement where he grew up. That one had been a real Army knife, used by his grandfather in WWII, a man he never got to meet.

Thoughts of the old basement brought back good as well as bad memories. He'd spent a lot of time there with his cat Princess. Fascinated by her primitive skills, he'd studied her with scientific detachment as she tore mice apart and ate them. She never showed remorse, and killing to survive was a lesson learned early on. One time, she'd brought him a mouse as a gift. So as not to insult her, he'd eaten and then vomited up the furry mess.

Using the skills Princess had taught him, he would

go hunting tonight. He had no choice if he were to stop the unrelenting voice, the one calling him a clumsy dolt with butter for brains and fat sausage fingers useless for creating the intricate designs she deserved.

"It wasn't my fault they took the hand before I could paint your nails." Why couldn't she understand?

Dropping the knife, he flung himself into a chair and cradled his head in his hands. There were times he wanted to cut her out of his brain. But then he would die.

At least he'd be with Princess.

Chapter Six

Hud turned over in bed, blindly reaching for the cell phone ringing annoyingly on the bedside table. The clock beside the phone indicated Tuesday: four thirty a.m. This boded ill.

Throwing back the covers, he rolled to a sitting position on the edge of the mattress. "Hey Marco, what's up."

"We found another one."

Hud scrubbed one hand across his face, then raked his fingers through his hair. "That makes number four."

"Four we're aware of."

"A chilling observation. Same M.O.?"

"To the letter. The newest victim is Georgia Tarkington, white female, thirty years old, dark brown hair, and works in a luxury spa. One open all night."

"How long ago, and who found the body?"

"According to forensics, less than three hours old. This one put up a fight. Found in LoDo by one of the people camped around there, who then reported the scene of horror to a convenience store clerk, who in turn phoned the police."

Lower Downtown Denver, aka LoDo, was a mixture of the old, the new, and the down and out. In other words, the area was a mashup of the good, the bad, and the dangerous. "Where's the body being taken?"

"The Bancroft Lab."

Hud's heart sank. Marilyn would be involved again.

"Forensics is still on the scene, but by the time you drive in, the body will be on its way.

"Then I'll meet you at Bancroft." Hud signed off, cleaned up, and threw on his clothes.

The stars struggled to shine through the dusky morning light, and a faint hint of brightness peeked up over the eastern horizon. Living on a farm, rising early was the norm, but four a.m. was early even for him.

Entering the barn via the walkthrough, Hud grabbed an armload of hay and opened the stall door to the first pen. His two Nubian goats, Jessabelle and Jubilee, leaped to their feet. Their expressions held alarm, their bodies tensed and ready to run. "Easy, ladies, it's me. Who else would be bringing your hay at this hour?"

Being prey animals, he supposed hyper-alertness was part of their DNA. He wished the women in the Denver area had the same survival instincts. The newspaper warned them to travel in groups and to avoid being out at night. But being strongminded and liberated they seemed to throw caution to the wind.

"Sorry about another down and dirty morning feed." He aimed his apology to his entire herd of confused animals as he doled out kibble and hay.

Half an hour later, with everyone fed and watered and the shoveling left for later, he put the dogs in charge and climbed into his 4x4.

A pang of sorrow for their new victim struck deep, and he stomped on the accelerator and sped down the country road leaving a cloud of dust blowing in the breeze.

****

Marco was waiting outside the autopsy room. The accommodations at the Bancroft facility were far superior to the outdated Denver county morgue. Here the floors leading to the double doors were made of travertine tile, and the walls were painted a comforting smoky blue, quietly ushering the dead to the final insult of being cut open and analyzed.

Hud hated this part of the job. As he hustled down the hallway, he noted Marco didn't appear anxious to join the proceedings either. They pushed through the swinging doors together and hovered by the wall. The autopsy was already underway.

The smell permeating the room reminded Hud of antelope hunting. At least when you dressed-out an animal, you had the great outdoors in which to work. Here, despite the fancy exhaust system, the concentrated raw guts and blood aroma managed to make its presence known.

Dr. Monrose worked at the head of the metal table. The woman who had been invading his thoughts of late stood gowned, gloved, and wearing a surgical cap as she carefully hooked electrodes to the victim's head. She appeared to be running an EEG strip similar to the one he'd seen at her lab. There was a gentleness in Dr. Monrose's touch and respect in the manner in which she handled the body.

Marilyn glanced up, and their gazes locked. Her eyes widened as if she was startled to see him at the morgue. He gave a little nod. She didn't respond in kind but quickly returned her attention to the task at hand.

On a nearby metal table, a second contraption sat beside the typical brainwave machine. Electrodes from this odd piece of equipment were also attached to the cadaver. The apparatus hummed and purred, and the front panel held a collection of blue lights blinking in a random pattern.

A few minutes later, her procedure apparently completed, Dr. Monrose packed up in record time and scooted out the far door which led to the decontamination area. She was in and out in a flash. He'd arrived a little late at the previous autopsies, no wonder he'd missed her on those occasions.

Marco gave him a nudge to the ribs with his elbow. "Go on, I'll wait for the prelim report."

Hud followed Dr. Monrose.

Minus the gown and wearing street clothes, she leaned over the large stainless-steel sink, scrubbing her hands and forearms as if preparing for open heart surgery.

She didn't acknowledge his presence.

"We need to talk." He grabbed a clean towel off a stack and held the white cotton out toward her.

As if resigned to her fate, she shut off the water and accepted his offering. When she turned to face him, he expected anger, or at least a good bit of irritation. But what he saw was akin to resignation, maybe even relief.

"Meet me at my lab." Not uttering another word, she slam-dunked the towel in the waiting bin, gathered her belongings, and left.

****

Hud stepped across the threshold and into Marilyn's lab. She waited for the security door to close and lock before she spoke.

"Let me remind you, PI Kincaid, all information you learn here is classified. In fact, I found out yesterday the Government has shown a passing interest in my work."

"Our government?"

"Yes, of course."

"Why?"

"I'm not aware of the specifics. But every application I can come up with sounds like Black Ops, or Army Intelligence, or something equally scary."

"That sounds ominous. Maybe you'd better explain to me exactly what you're doing?"

"If I take you into my confidence, you have to promise you won't tell anyone. If they find out I leaked even one iota of this information, I will disappear. And you might too."

"What do you mean by disappear?"

"I'll be transferred to a lab Heaven-knows-where to continue the work until it's completed or my contract is up. Hard telling what will happen to you."

This gave him pause. She sounded serious. But how could he rationalize being in possession of crucial information without sharing the data with the DPD—or at least with Marco?

"Promise me."

She was taking a leap of faith in trusting him, and the soulful pleading in her eyes made him want to comply. In fact, he wanted to promise her more than to keep his mouth shut. He wanted to promise her sunsets on the front porch and breakfast on the veranda. None of which was likely to happen anytime soon, if ever.

"Did you hear what I said?"

"I can't. I won't make promises I'm unable to keep." Where this case was concerned, he didn't have the luxury of trusting her in kind.

Her stance relaxed, and she gave a nod of acceptance. "Okay. At least that's an honest answer, which is more than I get around here lately. I'll defer to your discretion because I have to tell somebody."

Sliding two metal stools out from under the lip of the stainless-steel lab table, she sat on one and offered for him to take the other. "Sit down, and I'll explain the gist of what I'm doing."

As he followed her suggestion, he considered grabbing paper and pencil to take notes. Afraid of spooking her, he rejected the idea.

"Hopefully the data collected this morning will prove more useful than my past sessions."

Apparently filled with nervous energy, she gained her feet and paced about the small immediate area. "Working with these women has been the hardest project I've ever been on—in more ways than one."

She paused and stood facing him. "What happened to these women is ghastly, and heartbreaking." Her eyes were bright with tears, confirming to him she didn't view the victims as lab rats or simply a means to an end. "And regardless of what Kingsley hopes to get out of this, my goal now is to help find their killer."

"Then we're on the same team. Lately, this case has been the only thing on my mind—almost." Did she catch his drift? The fleeting quirky smile she didn't bother to hide seemed to indicate yes.

"Follow me."

"Anywhere."

"Oh, brother." Her words were accompanied by a

refined eyeroll.

Turning, she led him into a room housing an array of equipment Dr. Frankenstein would have coveted.

"To be honest, I stumbled on the electroencephalogram idea by accident."

As if working with a rare archaeological find, she carefully opened a large white envelope labeled Georgia Tarkington. Removing this morning's EEG strip, she fed the paper ribbon into one of her machines. After adjusting several dials, she tapped a switch setting the apparatus to softly humming.

"There are documented theories stating a body weighs less immediately after death, but what makes up the difference? The soul, the spirit, an unknown form of energy?" She shrugged. "Nobody is sure. Then I thought what if there was an undiscovered element in the brain following death. So, I started taking EEG's of deceased people."

"How long have you been working on this."

"Over two years."

Marilyn's clientele might be a little unusual, but her dedication was impressive. And Hud was relieved to learn her project wasn't a new age spur-of-the-moment idea dreamed up to spend grant money.

"The EEG information I've discovered is then manipulated through the programs I created. But I have to capture the data within twenty-four hours after death, or the process doesn't work.

"Live subjects, such as people in comas or regular healthy individuals, can be recorded successfully of course, but I don't believe the data gathered comes from the same area of the brain."

Marilyn appeared stuck on pondering this oddity.

Unable to offer up a constructive statement or a decent question to encourage her to continue, he nodded and cleared his throat. The sound seemed to bring her back to the present.

"The process is lengthy and convoluted. These pieces of paraphernalia interpret and then convert the EEG into a visual form. After running through another piece of equipment which I designed, the stream of data becomes virtual reality ready, able to be viewed through my souped-up headset."

"Slow down a minute, Einstein." He'd considered his ex-girlfriend Jennifer computer savvy, but what she'd taught him was child's play compared to this stuff. "So far what you've told me sounds like science fiction and definitely a discovery the Government would want in on. But haven't you come across any information that might be helpful to our case?"

She took a deep breath in and exhaled slowly. "I believe the murderer is a man."

"Why do you say that?"

"I saw a fleeting glimpse of the eyes and the size of the hands."

Her info jived with theirs. "The force needed to commit the murders and the angle of the wounds supports your idea and our conclusion the killer is male. What else?"

"So far that's all."

"Oh." He couldn't keep the disappointment from his voice. "When are you going to run the input from the newest victim?"

"I just started the conversion. The second process takes about a day and a half to prepare and to convert to the final phase. I think I'll need the time to screw up my courage to go through another session."

"What do you mean?"

"The experience lasts approximately three minutes. But they are three minutes of pure terror. The visions don't come from the victim's everyday random points of view. They are strictly made up of the last three minutes of their existence. And with VR, the experience is like it's happening to me."

That sounded horrible—and dangerous. "What is all this doing to your brain?"

"The first thing is the physical effect, usually nausea and vomiting, which isn't uncommon in full immersion virtual reality. Then on top of the expected increased levels of adrenalin, heartrate, and breathing, there is the emotional effect of shock and panic—and the slipping away into nothingness. In the end, they don't remember the pain."

She fell silent, her hands clasped tightly together, her lips pressed into a hard line as if to keep them from trembling. She appeared…heartbroken.

Hud covered the distance between them and gathered her into a gentle embrace. When she turned her face upward to him, he kissed her. He shouldn't have. He hardly knew this woman, but he felt a connection to her that defied logic. Those tempting lips relaxed, and she kissed him back.

Then Marilyn broke their connection and nestled her forehead against his chest. Arms still locked around her, he continued holding her, suppressing the urge to rock her back and forth as if he comforted a child.

Suddenly, she came to attention, nearly catching him on the chin with her head. Stepping back, she swiped at a tear on her left cheek. "That was totally unprofessional. I'm sorry." She straightened her lab coat and squared her shoulders.

"I'm not," he admitted. "And at times, the line between professional and personal gets blurred for all of us."

"Thank you for saying so."

The brief encounter left him wanting more, and although she didn't mention the kiss, he couldn't pass up the chance to do so. "What about lingering effects? I mean from your experiment, not from that great kiss."

She glanced away, not taking the bait to his inuendo. "Hard to explain."

"Try"

"Okay. Here goes. Recently, I'm getting random bursts of emotions and desires I don't recognize as my own. The impulses are no longer limited to the VR data centering around the death of the victims. This information has to do with their everyday lives. The source is a mystery, and preventing it is too."

She fell silent. Not wanting to crowd her, Hud retreated and leaned against the wall, arms crossed over his chest. "Go on," he encouraged.

"Do you recall at the restaurant when I asked if you had a dog?"

"Yes. And by the way, they did get a scrap of BBQ which they loved. Maybe someday you can come out and they can thank you in person."

"Maybe." Her distracted tone indicated she wasn't really aware of what she'd almost agreed to. "Anyway, the point being, growing up I had a little terrier named Heidi, but I don't have a dog now, and the idea of anything dog related hasn't crossed my mind in years. But besides being a vet assistant, LeAnn Swanson was a dog groomer."

"I guess I follow."

"Now dogs come to mind quite frequently. I almost bought dog food at the store the other day. And Becky Chapman worked at a bakery. I have been craving scones, and eclairs, and sweet rolls like you can't believe. Those are treats I allow myself once in a blue moon—and yes I know last month there was such a celestial occurrence."

She beat him to the punch on that one. "Maybe you can chalk it all up to a case of nerves. These visions sound horrendous, and you're more emotionally involved than any of us."

"Perhaps, but then why am I dancing around my kitchen when I cook. I mean literally leaping about. Becky was also studying to be a ballerina."

A deep sadness struck as Hud remembered the victim's bio having mentioned her taking dance lessons. "That is pretty specific. Anything else?"

"Sometimes when you look at me I get all giggly, like a schoolgirl. I figure the younger victims probably still believed in storybook romance, and crushes, and love at first sight."

"And you don't believe in any of those conditions of the heart."

"Of course not."

"Anybody trying to breathe life into an old Victorian house is a romantic. And it's hardly fair to blame your reaction to my charm and good looks on an unwanted side effect. Besides, when we kissed, I'm betting that was the real you."

"There could be a bit of overlapping of emotions on that one."

Her cheeks flushed, and she toyed with a diode or some weird electronic widget she picked up off the counter. "*A wise girl kisses but doesn't love and leaves before she is left.*"

"What?"

"Oh sorry, I didn't mean to spout a Marilynism."

"A Marilynism?"

"A quote from Marilyn Monroe, therefore a Marilynism. I freely admit to being a fanatic on the subject. My mother was obsessed with the movie star too, so I've been immersed in all things Marilyn since I was in the womb.

"She fought to be appreciated for her mind and to be taken seriously. I can relate. At times, the field of science remains a hard road for a woman to navigate."

Surprised by this outpouring of personal revelations, Hud remained silent, schooling his face into a nonjudgmental expression.

"Well, at least you're not ridiculing me."

"I found what you shared fascinating, not funny." Was he laying it on a little thick?

"Oh really? It's been a while since I've been found fascinating." Her tone was lighthearted, like she'd caught him pushing the envelope. She had good instincts.

"Tell me more about virtual reality. I'm not familiar with the VR scene other than when I drive by the local arcades." At his request, Marilyn's face lit up, and she eagerly enlightened him.

"VR has come a long way, but the basic premise is to magically trick your brain into believing you are in a 3D environment."

"Magically? That's a bit unscientific."

She gave a huff of irritation. “Maybe not magic, but the process is an amazing trick. By using simulated binocular vision, the apparatus presents slightly different images to each eye, giving the illusion a two-dimensional picture is actually three-dimensional. And my equipment goes beyond state of the art to futuristic.

“There are so many incredible uses for this technology—like visiting museums, learning to drive, learning surgical procedures, exploring countries you’ll never get a chance to visit. Or you can fly like a goose, or rock climb with a mountain goat. I like goats.”

“You like goats? Are you sure that’s the real you speaking?”

“Yes. The real me likes goats. They can be so Zen, sitting in the sun, chewing their cud, eyes at half-mast.”

“Ha, you haven’t met mine. Did you grow up on a farm?”

“Heavens no.” Her tone made the very idea sound like a tour in the Army or a stint at Ryker’s Island. “But in the summers, we visited my aunt and uncle in Michigan, on their dairy farm. Besides a herd of cows, they had goats to play with. I like cows too.”

Here was the country kitten he hoped she might be deep down inside. “Remind me to buy a cow.”

She giggled, and the sound harbored a good helping of the girlishness she’d previously mentioned. She shook her head. “How did we get from VR technology to bovines?”

“I not sure, but we should get back to the workings of the virtual world.”

“You’re right. In a nutshell the process mostly has to do with frames per second and how fast your GPU, the graphics processing unit, can display images. I’ve tweaked and rebuilt most of the equipment so I can't explain the changes in simple terms because they were far from simple. I'm still trying to eliminate the nausea and vomiting reaction."

"Ugh. Throwing up is the worst. Do the symptoms last long?"

"Long enough to keep me awake at night trying to figure out a way to counteract the effect."

"You're very dedicated to your work, aren't you?"

"I always have been. And now I'm driven by the need to help find the person committing these murders."

"Sounds like there's not much time left for relationships."

Marilyn canted her head slightly and studied him. "No, there isn't. At least not for anything serious…so far."

Did he detect the possibility of hope? Apparently having no intention of expanding on her reply, she launched back into her VR recitation.

"In an attempt to be an objective observer, on second replays I partially reversed the logic trying to redirect the emotions coming through. But no luck there either. Therefore, going through the secessions remains hard."

The computer into which she'd fed the EEG ribbon gave a demanding repetitive beep. Marilyn ran to the machine as if a bomb might go off if she didn't avert the countdown.

"Ready for phase two," she informed him over her shoulder.

Downloading the new data onto a flash drive, she installed the intel into a second machine. "This is the process I told you takes the longest. Most of the required time actually."

"And what will you be doing until then?"

"Paperwork, I'm afraid. Which I need to start right now."

Taking the hint, he prepared to leave. "When you're ready to go virtual with this new information I need to be here."

She contemplated the request, then gave an almost imperceptible nod. "To be honest, I'll be glad for the company."

Chapter Seven

Warren parked a short way up the street from Marilyn's house. Then he waited for true darkness.

Tonight, his rental car was a Ford Taurus. Quite the downgrade from his beloved BMW. He glanced around the interior of the screamingly ordinary vehicle. Only a soccer-mom van would be more embarrassing to drive. But since the fiasco last Saturday night, this was all he could afford.

He massaged his bruised shoulder. His ribs hurt too. The enforcer employed by the underground gambling parlor had worked him over but good—the unspoken message loud and clear, *Pay up soon or next time go down for the count.*

Maybe the underground casino was rigged. How could he have such bad luck three times running? Regardless, he needed Marilyn's help to save his ass.

Frustrated, he pounded his fists against the steering wheel. He'd have to forego picking up the new suit he'd ordered. He'd lose the deposit, but there was no way he could pay off the balance he owed. Truly, Marilyn was his last hope.

A light went on inside her house. It was about time she got home from work. She must have parked in the back and come in through the kitchen door.

He should have treated her better in the time they'd spent together, then her compliance might be more easily gained. He patted his jacket pocket, reassured by the bulk of the Ruger LCR. Lately, he'd felt the need for protection. Tonight, it would serve as persuasion, should Marilyn prove obstinate.

He'd purchased the firearm a week ago at a pawn shop. The store had been dark and smelly. A biohazard warning on the door wouldn't have come as a surprise. But they sold firearms under the table, no questions asked—what had he expected? Another transaction costing a pretty penny.

Palms sweating, stomach in an uproar, he screwed up his courage for what he was about to do. One way or another, he was leaving with vital data on Marilyn's project. He'd put out feelers and knew he could get a good price for the information.

Taking a deep breath, he opened the car door and slid out, then forced the panel silently closed. Head canted downward, he speed-walked to Marilyn's front door and rang the bell. Ignoring the impulse to pace the length of the porch, he waited for her to answer.

"Oh, it's you. Hi, Warren. Did we have a date I've forgotten about?"

"No, I just had the urge to come and surprise you. You sound disappointed, were you expecting someone else?"

"A girl can always hope."

"May I come in?" He shifted his weight from one foot to the other disregarding her subtle insult.

"I don't want to be rude, but it's been a long day, and I still have a ton of paperwork to do. Could we do this another night?"

"Not really."

Pushing his way inside, he closed the door at his

back. Marilyn's expression of surprise turned to one of anger.

"What the heck, Warren. You need to leave."

"Listen to me, dammit. I'm in trouble with some nasty people, and I need your help. Give me some of the info on your project, enough to sell my way out of the hole I'm in."

"I will not. How dare you even ask."

"Come on, for old time's sake." Why couldn't she understand this was literally a life-or-death situation.

"Our time together is hardly old, and certainly not worth my being fired over, or worse yet going to jail."

He slid the revolver from his pocket. "I'm afraid I must insist."

"Are you crazy? Put the gun away, Warren. Being a gangster doesn't suit you. You might get blood on your fancy clothes and shoes."

Stupid cow. She wasn't taking him seriously. He slapped her across the face with his free hand. Now he had her attention.

Holding one hand to her cheek, Marilyn backed away toward the room he knew as her library/home office. Good, unwittingly she was heading in the right direction. "Stand over there. Against the wall." When she followed his orders, he began rifling through the paperwork spread out on the desk.

"Who's the buyer? NeuroTronTech? Jade told me there'd been entities sniffing around. Oh Warren, why are you doing this?"

"You certainly are full of questions."

"Don't I have the right to know why you're pointing a gun at me?"

"Not really. And I wouldn't be pointing anything

other than my dick at you if you weren't such a goody-two-shoes, and you'd help me willingly." She didn't crack a smile at his joke. What a bitch. "Where's the good stuff? I won't get much for this drivel."

"It's at work."

"Liar. I've seen you drag half your office home at night locked in your briefcase." He surveyed the room but didn't spot her blasted carryall.

In pure frustration, he kicked at the desk. Things were not going in his favor. He needed money to pay off his debt to the Colorado Cowboy Mafia, or at least enough to stall them until he could activate his last resort contingency plan. And that would cost plenty too. Changing his identity and slipping off to a foreign country without extradition wouldn't come cheap.

Anger replaced frustration. He turned to question Marilyn, ducking in the nick of time to avoid the large science manual sailing toward his head.

"Nice try." Striding across the room, he grabbed her by the hair and smashed her against the wall. "I'm not kidding around. I'm a desperate man, willing and capable of doing desperate things."

****

"You win, Warren," Marilyn uttered through clenched teeth. "Let me go."

He complied by shoving her away from his body and into the desk chair.

Fighting to maintain a seated position, she grabbed ahold of the padded arms as the chair-on-wheels skidded to one side.

Marilyn knew her coworker used ruthless methods to screw with his competition as he fought his way up the corporate ladder, but this was a whole new level of cold-bloodedness. An unexpected and extremely dangerous level. Whatever his reasons, she wasn't about to let him have the data. She had to try and talk him out of this crazy scheme.

"You didn't answer my question," she prodded. "Who's paying you, NeuroTronTech?"

"They were willing to pay the most."

"But they're notorious for working with foreign countries, especially China. And they love leaking info to the press."

"So what? When you inform Kingsley of what's happened, the Institute will take out a patent on your work, and your grant money will be safe."

"Warren, there's more at stake here than patents and money."

"Such as."

Should she tell him about the search for the serial killer? Trusting to his humanitarian side seemed foolhardy, if ever he had one. Now she wished she hadn't said anything.

"Such as what?" Warren screamed out the words, spittle flying from his snarling mouth. He was becoming more and more unhinged.

The doorbell rang. They both jumped and stood staring at one another.

"You expecting anyone?"

"Yes," she lied, "so you'd better get out of here, Warren."

"Who," he challenged.

"An officer from the DPD is supposed to pick up my findings from today's autopsy. I'm working with them."

"Working with them on what?

"I'm trying to help them find the serial killer."

"You're kidding. That might up the ante on selling your information."

The bell rang again, accompanied to a very insistent pounding on the front door.

"Whoever it is, they won't be getting these."

Warren grabbed a handful of papers off her desk and stuffed them in his pockets. Familiar with the layout of the house, he sprinted for the back door. Marilyn ran in the opposite direction.

Flinging open the front door, she fell into PI Kincaid's arms.

"Whoa there, darlin'. What's the matter?"

"A business colleague of mine just burst in here trying to get his hands on my work."

"Where is he?"

"Out the back door. He's got a gun."

Weapon in hand, Hudson took the front steps two at a time and headed for the side yard. The noise of a car starting and the engine revving brought him up short. Warren must have already made it to the street.

Hudson reversed course and ran toward the sound and the danger. Jumping the curb and tires screeching, the Ford Taurus barreled toward him. The speeding vehicle missed him by inches before veering back onto the street and into the night.

Hanging onto the open front door, Marilyn tried to reason properly. If Hudson hadn't shown up, would Warren have shot her? She couldn't wrap her mind around the idea. Thank goodness her lie about someone stopping by from the DPD had been surprisingly close to the truth.

What was Hudson doing here anyway? With his

cowboy hat and perfect timing, PI Kincaid created quite an impressive image as he came to her rescue.

Weapon hanging down at his side, Hudson stood unmoving as Warren's car became a blur of taillights. Holstering his automatic, he retrieved his cell phone. "Marco. Yes, I realize you're on the job, but this is important."

Stepping farther away to continue his conversation, he turned his back to her, and Marilyn could no longer make out what he was saying. Turning, he pocketed the phone and strode across the lawn and up onto the porch. "Let's go inside."

Without waiting for agreement, he escorted her in and closed the door. Cupping her chin, he turned her face first one way then the other, and a small growl escaped him. "You should put ice on that bruise."

In the excitement she'd forgotten Warren had struck her. She must look awful, which seemed a silly thing to be worrying about as Hudson followed her to the kitchen.

"What was the phone call about?" Digging in the freezer, she retrieved a bag of frozen peas and smacked it on the counter to loosen the icy mass. Holding the package to her cheek, she sat down. Hudson took a seat too.

"I put a BOLO out on your friend Warren Jameson."

"What's a BOLO? And how did you know the man in the car was Warren?"

"After discovering Kingsley's connection to Bancroft and the autopsies, I did a routine check on several employees at the Institute. Warren Jameson being one of them. And a BOLO is a be on the lookout for. There was enough light from the streetlamp to recognize the low-life as he tried to run me over."

The reality of what had happened finally took hold. The bag of peas slipped from her grasp landing in her lap. Elbows propped on the table, she cradled her throbbing head in her hands and fought back tears, her emotions off the charts. Having her experiments already screwing with her brain, she didn't need this nightmare added to the mix.

"Aaa… Miss Marilyn can I get you anything? Tea, a drink, a Kleenex."

Sniffing, she sat up straight and blew out a big breath. "I'm good. You saved me from a truly dangerous situation. That's more than enough heroism for one night. You probably need to get home."

"I'm not going anywhere. I dropped by just to make sure we were still on for tomorrow afternoon—now it looks like I'd best hang around until morning."

Several hot scenarios raced through her mind. But she was tired, and if she looked like she felt—every hint of a romantic notion dissolved away. "No, really. You don't need to stay."

"No, really," he parroted back, sounding as stubborn as she was being. "I'm staying the night." He gained his feet and glanced around. "Which way to the couch?" She stood across the table from him. "Have you had supper?"

"No."

"I've got zucchini torte, salad, and pumpkin soup. Will that do?"

He swallowed hard as if the menu she described stuck in his throat. "Sounds great. Thank you. Speaking of food, I need to arrange for my neighbor to make sure my animals get their supper tonight too."

"Oh, of course. You said you had two dogs. Go ahead. I'll start heating things up."

As she washed her hands, and got out plates, bowls, and silverware, she eavesdropped on his call.

"Howdy, Buck. Yeah, it's me, Hud. Something unexpected happened, and I can't get back up there tonight." There was a pause as he listened to his friend. "It's kind of hard to explain."

She glanced over her shoulder, catching his intense gaze. With a flutter in her heart, she quickly busied herself back at the stove and microwave.

"Don't let the goats sweet talk you into giving them treats, just hay. And the horse and donkey have to eat separately. I know it's not your first rodeo. You're a good friend. I owe you. Oh, and make sure the gate latches shut, or the dogs will get out. Thank you. See you sometime tomorrow."

Apparently, PI Kincaid had more than a couple of dogs. "Sounds like you have quite the animal habitat."

"I reckon I do when you tally them all up. One way or another, stray animals seem to find me." He appeared quite happy about the predicament. "Where might I wash up?"

"End of the hall, on your right. This will be ready shortly," she added, as he turned to follow her directions.

She needed a drink. There was plenty of wine in the basement. Then again, maybe not. While she'd like to get to know Hudson better, after Warren's betrayal and threats, she probably needed a clear head and to keep this night strictly platonic. Besides, Hudson collaborated with the police, and he considered her a person of interest regarding the case. He may still think her somehow involved.

"Smells great. Thank you for feeding me, especially since I invited myself to stay."

Not having heard Hudson return, Marilyn tensed at the sound of his voice. She really could use a drink. "You're welcome. I'm fortunate you stopped by."

To sooth her frazzled nerves, yet not cloud her judgement, she switched on the radio to the channel playing torch songs from the '30s.

****

Marilyn flipflopped in bed, eyes wide open, sleep eluding her. The idea of Hudson staying downstairs on her couch was exciting as well as reassuring.

The time she'd spent with him at the kitchen table had been nice. A little awkward on occasion, but nice. He'd even helped tidy up. But as they'd both steered clear of personal information, Hudson Kincaid PI pretty much remained a mystery. There was a rugged outdoorsy appeal about him. And he seemed laid back the majority of the time, even introspective on occasion.

She'd been so frightened earlier tonight and had lucked out when he showed up at the house. Warren had really gone off the deep end, sending the world around her slipping one notch farther beyond her understanding and control. Her inner turmoil wasn't in much better shape.

There had been one subject she and Hudson had discussed and reaffirmed. Tomorrow, Hudson would come to her lab and stay with her when she ran the results for Georgia Tarkington.

Thoughts of that arrangement produced a different set of mixed emotions to gnaw on. Suffering through the procedure one more time would take all the determination she could muster. So, on the good side, with Hudson there she wouldn't be able to chicken out. Conversely, having Hudson see her freaked out, nauseated, and most likely vomiting, didn't sound good at all. What would he think, seeing her at her worst?

With a yawn, she snuggled deeper under the covers. If she didn't get some sleep, her worst might be the face in the mirror come the morning.

Chapter Eight

Lying in the unmade bed, Archie took comfort this morning in staring up at his new prize dangling overhead. She'd been easy to spot in the dark, wearing her white coat like a uniform of virtue. White to hide the black in her heart.

At the memory of all the cruelty and deceit, a growl of anger slipped out, making his head hurt worse. The sound plummeted to the ground as if weighed down by the sadness and discontent hovering in the gloomy cellar.

Sitting up, Archie covered his ears with his hands, trying to stop the buzzing in his brain. The noise, like a thousand bees, didn't recede. Sometimes gliding his hands back and forth across his smooth head helped. He'd never grown any hair—anywhere. This angered his mother too. Working at a beauty salon, she declared his bald as a cue ball head brought her endless shame and taunting. Nothing he did was ever good enough for her.

The boys at school had been equally as mean, calling him Archibaldy Underpants rather than Archie Underwood. And the girls were even worse. Screaming and running away when he tried to talk to them. They didn't run away anymore, at least not far.

Turning his head slowly so as not to increase the near unbearable throbbing, he glanced at the bottles of nail polish he'd dug out of the trash bin behind the salon up the street.

Each bottle contained barely enough polish to paint one hand—that's all he'd need.

****

Following a restless night on Marilyn's couch, Hud vacated her place at the crack of dawn.

The chemistry between the two of them had seemed obvious. Too bad there'd been no experimenting to find out what kind of explosion they were capable of setting off. Or maybe playing it cool was for the best.

When he'd gotten home this morning, he'd found Buck already doing chores. As they finished up, his neighbor informed him the previous evening when he came over to feed, he'd found the dogs trapped in the barn, and the door to Hud's house unlocked and partway open.

Checking things out, Hud found nothing missing. But his computer was on, and someone had snooped through the papers on his desk. Due to power surges, Hud generally shutdown his computer when he left the house. Maybe the intruder had been a hitchhiker or a drifter. His property wasn't far off some major crossroads.

The dogs being in the barn was a puzzler though. They were top notch guard animals, and they seemed tuckered out today. He'd better go back to not only closing but locking the main gate. Fences and gates didn't stop a determined prowler, but they did slow them down so you could take better aim.

During the morning, he checked in with the DPD task force for new intel, of which there was none, and he caught up on shoveling in the barn. Now, as he drove back to Denver to meet Marilyn at the Kingsley Institute, he shook his head and smiled at the bright pink travel mug with the Gucci logo stuck in his truck cup-holder.

Up early this morning and dressed like a fashionista, Marilyn insisted on making and giving him coffee for the road as he headed out the door. She seemed a contradiction unto herself wearing those high heels and height of fashion clothing when her home was filled with antiques, and books on gardening, and how to cook on a woodstove.

****

Marilyn wrung her hands as she tried to decide if she were more nervous about the upcoming procedure or the fact Hudson would soon be here to observe the grueling display.

The lengthy conversion process was finally done. All the data had gone through the programing phase without a hitch, leaving no excuse for a delay or a reason to call him and cancel.

Changing from heels and a flattering skirt, she donned yoga pants, sneakers, and a long-sleeved cotton pullover. An image of Marilyn Monroe's face from Some Like It Hot adorned the T-shirt. The garment, a favorite, had cost plenty. She didn't often wear the top, but doing so always bolstered her mood, which she could use today.

Out of habit, she grabbed her white lab coat. Then deciding against the idea of adding any extra layer in which to get tangled, she set the jacket aside.

The security buzzer sounded, and she jerked to attention. Okay, Norma Jean, it's show time.

Keying in the code, she hauled open the door to her inner sanctum, and there he was in all his rowdy cowboy glory. Today Hudson wore Levi's, boots, a plaid shirt, and a denim jacket. The nearly ever-present hat, of course, was the clincher.

"Good afternoon, Miss Marilyn."

"We can only hope."

He shrugged out of the jacket and removed his hat. She nodded toward a set of clothes hooks on the wall to the right.

Did he persist in calling her Miss Marilyn simply as a sweet countrified gesture? Or did the words keep up a tiny barrier preventing them from becoming overly familiar. He sounded preoccupied, and whatever closeness they'd shared last evening seemed to have dissolved away.

"Come along then, PI Kincaid. I guess we'd best get started." She could play it cool too.

"Are you sure you're ready for this?"

His voice held concern. Maybe her mood had changed, not his.

"I'm as ready as I'll ever be."

"Then besides staying out of your way, what do you want me to do?"

"I'll put on the equipment and sit in the reclining chair in the side cubby. From there on it's pretty unchoreographed."

Several cables ran from the computer to the chair. Arm and leg straps hung off the sides. She wouldn't use the restraints today, or ever again. The first time she employed them, the results were unanticipated and painful. Bruised and battered from struggling, she'd nearly broken her arm. While reliving the victim's last three minutes, she wasn't cognizant of her true self, didn't comprehend how to loosen the straps or protect her body.

The recently added padding to the walls and floor should be sufficient to cushion her body as she fought the killer and fell dead to the ground. Nothing protected her brain from the assault about to take place.

"Unless I'm truly in danger, don't try to stop what's about to happen." She harnessed up the equipment and gave the thumbs up sign.

The computer hummed, and the converter appeared properly set. With the hyped-up headgear in place, she sat in the chair—a false moment of comfort. If only she were taking a break instead of jumping into the nightmare recollections of Georgia Tarkington. Reaching sideways, she hit the main switch. Let the horror begin.

Pain exploded in her head, she staggered then turned and ran. Someone had struck her a blow from behind. She hadn't seen anyone hiding in the shadows.

Keep running, don't look back. One more block to go, one block to a street where someone can help me. She fled into the night, legs pumping furiously, anger fueling her body more than fear. Did he want her money? She threw down her purse. He didn't take the bait. At least without the extra weight she could run faster. He labored behind her, breathing hard as he tried to keep up.

Pain erupted in her back—deep searing pain. Had she been shot? She hadn't heard gunfire. The agony brought her to her knees. No, no, no she had to keep moving. Crawl away, crawl away.

He growled like an animal, circling around her.

The pain got worse. Now she couldn't breathe. Her mouth was full of blood. Choking and vomiting she heaved and gasped, then landed facedown. What was happening? She felt so weak. She couldn't move.

He drew near. Run, run, get up and run. Why wouldn't her body listen. He hovered over her. What felt like a foot came down on the small of her back, crushing her hips into the dirt. He grunted, then stepped back. The pain changed, felt almost better. Still coughing up blood, she rolled to one side and stared up at him. He held a knife, drenched in blood—her blood. The knife had caused the pain, plunged deep in her back before he'd torn the blade free.

His other hand snaked out reaching for her throat. She knocked his arm aside and clawed his face with her nails. His hat tumbled to the ground. His grotesque face loomed closer. A far-off streetlight illuminated the shiny dome of a bald head and the tattoo on the side by his ear. She grabbed at his clothing. Can't get a grip. Slick, cold, not real—how could any of this be real?

So tired. Can't move. He's straddling my hips. I can't push him off. The sound of an animal roaring jolted her back momentarily from the world into which she'd happily retreated. A knife flashed before her eyes. Pain, pain, terrible pain.

Let go… Slip away… Everything's all right. They're waiting.

The hard floor of the lab hurt Marilyn's knees, yet the pain came as a comfort because she knew the session was over. Yanking off the headgear, she crushed the equipment to her chest and tried to calm her erratic breathing. Then pushing the apparatus aside, she crawled over to the waste bin and vomited. Thank goodness she'd positioned the container closer.

Hudson crouched at her side. Forgetting he was in the room, she jumped as he held out a fistful of wet paper towels. Grabbing them, she buried her face in the cool relief. "Thank you."

"That was horrible to witness. I can't imagine what you saw from the inside. Are you going to be okay?"

"Eventually. Each time, the process seems to take more out of me."

They both remained silent.

Laboring to breathe, she sucked in a lungful of cleansing air and blew it out and felt better. "Until I can manage to withstand the replay as a whole, what I saw will come back in pieces. Oh quick, help me up. I saw a useful image. I need paper and pencil, get me to my desk.

Hudson lifted her up, carried her across the room, and set her in the office chair. She pawed at the desk in an unsuccessful attempt to open the drawer. The connection between her brain and body kept short-circuiting, and she twitched as if given small electrical shocks.

Gathering the items requested, he placed them within her reach. She stared at the paper. The details of what she'd seen began to fade. She squinted, and concentrated harder.

Without her asking, Hudson handed her a glass of water. Her mind remained befuddled, but her body responded to his kindness. She remembered the kiss they'd shared, wanted another. Super energized, her emotions were all over the place. As the odor from the trash bin wafted closer, the urge dwindled. She'd vomited in front of him. He may never want to kiss her again.

Gripping the edge of the desk with both hands, she forced her scrambled thoughts back on track and willed the images to resurface of their own accord.

As previously agreed, Hudson had withheld the details from Georgia Tarkington's autopsy and forensic report. By doing so, the official information couldn't influence the fatal recollections. After she explained what she'd seen in the VR session, Hudson would have to take them at face value, and she would have ambient information as well.

"Thank you for the water. I feel better. Grab a chair, and I'll tell you what I saw."

He settled in beside her. "Are you sure? You're pale as a ghost."

"Pretty fitting wouldn't you say."

He didn't smile at her attempt at levity.

"I'm going to record this. It's for my records only, but in case anyone else gets a hold of or confiscates the material, don't say anything you don't want the world to hear."

He nodded. "I got it."

She gave the date and time, then began. "The following are details for session number four, subject's name, Georgia Tarkington." To Marilyn, Georgia was much more than a cog in the wheel, and she disliked using such verbiage. But when dealing with theories, to have her work taken seriously demanded she be as scientific as possible.

Gaining an almost trance-like state, the words began to flow. "Georgia was a brave young woman. She fought tooth and nail…until the end. I hope they took samples under her fingernails. She scratched the killer's face.

"They should have found a head injury, fairly serious, but not lethal. Also, a wound in her back, from a knife. This was serious. Most likely resulting in a punctured lung, and possibly a severed vein or artery. But the fatal wound was the direct stab to the heart." She switched off the recorder, stifled a guttural sob, and pressed her fingertips to her eyes to prevent the tears from falling. Then gathering her faculties, she continued off the record.

"She fought so hard, Hudson. And Georgia felt like prey being hunted. Oh, there's more coming back." Marilyn punched the record button. "The subject tore at the attacker's clothing but felt something slippery like plastic not fabric. And she knocked his hat off. He's bald headed, completely. He has a tattoo." She retrieved the pencil and started drawing, her motions jerky while her coordination continued to return in fits and starts. "Like this. Two words. Cat Man."

"Bat Man?"

"No. Cat Man. The rendering is crude. Like a child scribed the letters."

Nausea swept through her again. Dropping the pencil, she gripped her stomach. "I can't do any more right now. Does what I've told you so far jive with the autopsy report?"

"Yes. You accurately described all three of the wounds—head, back, and chest. Also, you're correct about the stab to the heart being the fatal blow. Did you see his face?"

"Not in detail. But I know he is bald, and I mean completely bald."

"That's a great clue. And so is the tattoo. There's a

national police program cataloging tattoos of felons who have done or are doing time."

"What about forensics from the nail scrapings?"

"The recorder is off, right?"

"Yes. Why?"

"I'm about to tell you a critical piece of intel which hasn't been released to the public. And the information needs to stay hush hush. Got it?"

"Yes, of course. I promise."

"Which hand did she use to scratch the killer?"

Marilyn closed her eyes for a moment before answering. "I'm sure she used her right hand."

"This psycho has been cutting off one hand on each of the victims—the right one."

"Oh, mercy." Revolted by the information, she doubled over and buried her face in her hands—her two wonderful, beautiful, hands. She tried to imagine not having both and felt all the worse. Why would he do such a thing?

With a major effort, she straightened and swept her hair back from her face, tucking it behind her ears. "I didn't live through any such mutilation with any of the VR experiences. He must remove the hand after they're dead."

"The autopsies agree, the mutilation is postmortem. And this time, by design or friggin' dumb luck, the mad man we're chasing eliminated our first good chance to get DNA."

Marilyn tried to stand, got woozy, and sat back down.

"We need to get you home."

"But I need to make notes while things are still fresh in my mind, and there's the closed-circuit video of the procedure I need to review."

Hudson glanced around as if checking for the cameras.

"I'm sorry. I meant to tell you about the recording."

"No matter. Come on. You can make notes on the way and work on the CCTV video after you're home and have eaten." The expression on PI Kincaid's face didn't leave room for debate. Besides she was too wiped-out to argue.

Chapter Nine

As Hud drove, he kept glancing over at Marilyn.

Curled up in the passenger seat of his truck and leaning against the door, she appeared small and vulnerable.

Apparently, what she experienced during the process cost her a part of her life too. Quite the weighty cloak to wear on such slim shoulders,

Not interfering during the throes of the simulation had been hard to do—and hard to take. She'd be a mass of bruises and sore muscles tomorrow. And to think she'd gone through this ordeal not once, but three times.

Dr. Marilyn Monrose was a tough little lady. A physician with computers, Tesla-like machines, and deceased persons as patients—but a doctor none the less. He never would have pictured her in such a job.

He glanced over again. She was so wasted she could barely see straight. Yet even with her hands trembling and weaving about, she tried to focus and key information into her iPhone. A drunk on a bender would have had better luck. Would the data even make sense to her in the morning? He admired her persistence and could relate to her dog-with-a-bone work ethics.

She'd nailed the autopsy results—and given them two bits of information to run with.

While she'd gathered her data and closed up the

lab, he'd texted Marco about the suspect being bald, sending along a snapshot of the tattoo Marilyn had drawn. Tracking down the artwork would take time and luck, but they were better off than a few hours ago.

Before witnessing her experiment firsthand, he'd questioned the validity of her theory and her ability to aid their cause.

"We're here." He eased to a stop in front of Marilyn's house.

Her head snapped up, and she glanced around as if she had no idea where here might be.

He got out, went around to her side of the vehicle, and opened the door. She slid out and made an ungainly attempt to walk. Grabbing her arm, he shut the truck door and escorted her up onto the front porch. She poked around in her purse, searching for the door key which was right on top. Retrieving it, he opened the door and managed to get her into the house and then to the kitchen before she collapsed in a heap onto the nearest chair.

Not waiting for direction or permission, he began cooking. Late afternoon, yet early for supper, a light meal would do. Since there wasn't much in her fridge other than the basics, he opted for a scrambled egg and cheese sandwiches, like Uncle Louie used to make for him. Back then the meal would have come with a side of sausage or bacon or both. Uncle Louie loved his meat.

Cooking with speed rather than neatness, the sandwiches were ready in record time. Making one more forage into the fridge, he found a bag of salad fixin's and a can of sliced peaches. Opening the fruit, he drained the liquid into a glass, then set the peach slices on a bed of lettuce beside each sandwich and served up the food.

"Thank you. I didn't realize I was so hungry. And thirsty too." She reached for the fork with more enthusiasm than he expected. "Would you please bring me about a gallon of water?"

At least she still had her sense of humor. In the cupboard beside the sink, he found an old porcelain pitcher which he filled and brought to the table along with two large glasses. Apparently, she used her antiques. The idea appealed to him. Unless unique or quite expensive, he advocated the use of old items—they gave off memories as they made new ones.

For a while, silence captured the mood, and Hud was almost done eating when he remembered she'd taped the session. "I wasn't aware you videoed the experiment." He didn't appreciate being recorded without his knowledge.

"It's for my eyes only. You sound worried. Did you grab my backside when I was preoccupied?"

"The idea crossed my mind."

She laughed at his comment. "I'd rather be fully cognizant for any such event, thank you." Her suggestive sideways glance indicated she might have been open to the idea.

Several lusty scenarios hurtled through in his mind, and before saying anything stupid, he gained his feet and began cleaning up the kitchen.

"He cooks, he cleans, he fights for law and order. How come there's not a cowgirl hanging off your arm?"

"There was a somebody, but she was the farthest thing from a cowgirl." Not pleased by the memory, he vigorously scrubbed the frying pan. "Our trails went separate ways."

"Oh, sorry. I shouldn't have pried."

"Don't be," he countered. "Our parting company was the best thing to happen in a long while. And it leaves me open for new possibilities."

"Am I a possibility?"

He placed the cast iron pan on the stove and turned on a low flame for a quick dry. "That's up to you." The flame racing through his body was much hotter.

She seemed to consider his statement, and gaining her feet, she picked up her plate and glass and placed them in the sink beside which he stood.

They faced one another, and without preamble, a rough demanding kiss followed. He forgot about Marilyn's injuries as he pulled her close. She winced once but didn't stop kissing him back or slow her exploration of the buttons on the front of his shirt.

Reaching over, he flipped the gas off on the stovetop. Then he walked her backward out of the kitchen to the foot of the stairs which lead up to her bedroom. They'd only known one another for a week, but the powerful feelings they'd both been holding back seemed to have reached critical mass.

When they halted, she took one step up, making them equal in height. He studied her face. The desire in her eyes and the coquettish come-hither tilt of her head had him struggling to hit the brakes on the growing need.

"What about your notetaking and reviewing the video?" He didn't intend to listen later to complaints about how he'd distracted her, interrupting the timeline of her work.

"I don't care."

"And you're not just flying high from being zapped full of VR energy?

"Possibly, but don't be a buzzkill."

"That's what I was hoping you'd say."

He kissed her again, gently this time, savoring the moment rather than gobbling her up like a starving man.

Hands on his chest, Marilyn eased away from him. "Do you smell smoke?"

Was that a euphemism indicating his kisses were setting her on fire?

Turning his head to the side, he gave a good sniff. He knew he'd turned off the kitchen stove, but there really was a hint of smoke in the air.

Searching for the source, they followed the trail of the acrid odor. The smell grew strongest by the basement door. Marilyn reached for the doorknob. Grabbing her wrist, Hud held her back. With his other hand, he felt the wooden panel. "It's hot. Don't open it. Call 911."

While she made the call, he located three towels in the kitchen. After wetting them in the kitchen sink, he crammed them along the crack under the basement door stopping the smoke now seeping out in earnest.

"You had better gather your data and anything you can't live without. We need to get out of here. Is there a basement window close to a garden hose?"

"Yes, on the west side of the house." She pointed out the direction.

Following her instructions, he raced toward the back door. "Get a move on," he hollered back at her.

The basement window he sought was wide open.

The screen had been torn off and cast aside. Through the opening, he heard the crackle and saw the flickering light of an out-of-control fire. No use feeding O2 to the flames. He slid the window almost shut. Spying the garden hose on his right, he turned the spigot on full blast, then threaded the hose through the small opening he'd left. If they couldn't contain the fire to the basement, this old house was bound to go up quickly.

As he hurried back to the front of the house, he heard sirens in the distance.

Two pieces of Marilyn's equipment sat on the front porch, along with a briefcase and a duffle bag jammed full of folders and papers—but no Marilyn. Calling her name, he went inside and caught sight of her at the top of stairs.

A small box tucked under one arm, she also lugged a large, framed photo as she struggled on the steps. Halfway down, the board beneath her foot flipped loose and she stumbled. As she careened toward him, Hud seized the picture frame in one hand and wrapped his free arm around her waist with the other. Keeping them both upright, they half-walked, half-stumbled down to the landing and solid footing.

Wide-eyed, Marilyn clung to him. He glanced down. Swirling and dancing around their feet, smoke leaked up through the cracks in the old wooden floorboards.

****

Hud and Marilyn sat in the truck watching the battle of wills fought between the deadly flames and the brave men working to put them out.

The firemen won the war, but the fire claimed several skirmishes before the final retreat. The basement was nearly a total loss, as was one wall of the main floor library. The support beams may have been weakened too, and the Fire Chief declared her home unfit for habitation until a structural engineer checked and signed off on all safety concerns.

Addressing his personal worries, Hud used his cell phone to call his neighbor. “Hi Buck. Yeah, you guessed it, I’ll be late to feed. She really is. Thanks again.”

“What did he say?” Knees up, her arms wrapped around her legs, Marilyn appeared at home occupying the passenger seat. He liked seeing her there. Too bad the circumstances were so dire.

“Buck said he’d wander over after his chores and do mine, so no rush getting there. He also said, and I quote, ‘She must really be somethin’.’ I agreed with him.”

“Do you mean it?”

“I do.”

“Thank you for that. I can’t believe this is happening.”

He nodded toward the house. “Anything in there you can’t live without tonight?”

“No, I suppose not.” She sat up straighter and reached to open the door of the truck. “I took a cab to work this morning in case I didn’t feel like driving home. Thank goodness the fire didn’t reach the garage. Now we can load everything in my car, and I’ll get a room at one of the hotels on Colorado Boulevard.”

“You’re staying at my place tonight. You shouldn’t be alone.”

“But you’ve done so much already and…”

“I really don’t mind.”

"Okay, and thank you. I can follow you in my car. After what's happened, I don't want to leave it here unattended for any length of time. Besides, the drive will give me time to get my thoughts in order and physically reach some kind of equilibrium."

"Are you sure you're up to driving?" The idea was sensible, and with her own car available she wouldn't feel stranded at his house. Yet he needed to be certain she could make the trip without getting woozy.

"The food you made revived me. But keep me in your rearview mirror. Okay? I have a terrible sense of direction, especially outside the city. If you lose me, you may never see me again."

"I'd never let that happen."

Chapter Ten

Amazed she'd driven this far, tired as she was, Marilyn yawned and watched Hudson open the gate to his property.

When he returned to his truck, she put her car in gear and followed him up a dirt road toward a small log home. Barking joyfully, two dogs ran alongside his vehicle.

They parked the vehicles side by side, and she got out and breathed in the crisp clean air. The effect boosted her energy. Glancing up took her next breath away. The night sky held an uncountable number of stars, like diamonds casually tossed across the heavens from horizon to horizon. On her right, the soft glow of an artificial light could be seen far off across the prairie. She guessed the infamous Buck lived there.

"It's beautiful. And so quiet." She whispered the words as if the sound might intrude on the magical setting.

"Enjoy the silence while you can. The frogs on the pond ought to be starting up any minute, serenading one another. They can be a noisy lot. But everything has its season. There won't be many nights of their music left to enjoy before a cold snap sends them hibernating for the winter."

Marilyn wasn't sure how far they'd driven, but compared to hers, Hudson's place felt like a parallel universe. As she took it all in, a shiver raised the hair on the nape of her neck, marring the beauty of the moment. She was standing in the dark with PI Kincaid because back in her universe her house had been set on fire.

Her spirits slumped along with her shoulders. Poor house. Just when she'd made a bit of progress restoring the old girl. The insurance would pay for repairs, but her mental status might be a lost cause. Spiritually, she wasn't convinced she could start over. Even some of the shrubs and flowers she'd broken her back planting were ruined by necessity as the firemen saved the dwelling. But enough with the negative thinking. She was tired. Surely things would seem better in the morning.

Hudson pressed a box of her project information into her arms and then helped her to gather the more important items to take inside.

"Are you sure the fire was deliberate?"

Hudson didn't answer until he'd unlocked the door and settled her inside.

"The fire chief sounded pretty convinced. Forensics will get a better handle on things in the morning when they investigate in the light of day."

"I can't imagine who would do this."

"How about Warren. Did he seem angry enough to plot revenge for your not helping him?"

"I'm not sure…I don't think so…I don't know. He seemed desperate, waving that gun around, babbling about being in a life-or-death situation. But to burn down my house. That's pretty extreme."

"When I spoke with Marco earlier today, he said Warren was known to visit an illegal gambling outfit they've had under surveillance. If he's involved, he's playing with high rollers, and they don't take IOU's. They probably have connections in Vegas, so he truly may be in trouble with a capital T."

"Wow. No wonder he acted irrationally. But we could have died in the fire. How does that benefit Warren?"

"You got me. I'm throwing out scenarios, not accusations."

He glanced at the framed picture they'd set off to one side. "You nearly took a bad fall on those stairs trying to save your memorabilia."

"If you hadn't been there, I'd have taken a header, for sure. The board suddenly coming loose seems odd."

"When we're allowed back in, we have to remember to make repairs on that step and check the other as well."

"I feel like more than just my house is falling apart."

"You've definitely been through some major changes recently." Hudson placed his right hand on her shoulder, then traced a path down her arm to her hand, entwining his fingers with hers. "You'll get through this, Marilyn. One step at a time, pun intended. Now grab your overnight gear and follow me."

Releasing her hand, he turned and led the way to the back of the house. "I inherited this property only recently, so there's still remodeling to be done."

"Like my place—or what's left. I'll feel right at home."

Constructed to show off the logs inside and out, the house was surprisingly roomy. Skylights promised sunshine during the day, and the effect created a delightfully homey atmosphere.

Hudson ushered her along the short hallway. "When Uncle Louie was alive, this was my room. Now I have his, so I guess my room is the guest room. Calling it that sounds weird."

"I'm sorry you lost your uncle."

"Thank you. We spent many notable times together."

"Do you have brothers and sisters?"

"Two brothers, both older. We had fun growing up, but now we're scattered across the country.

Marilyn's family tree was more of a sturdy stalk. No grandparents, and only one uncle way up in Michigan, so basically just mom and dad. They loved her dearly, and she loved them, but growing up had been a lonely business.

Her parents worked hard, but she knew they had struggled financially to see to her education. She'd paid them back but felt guilty she hadn't returned to Illinois to visit them recently. They seemed happy, the two of them on their own, and they'd always encouraged her to try her wings.

She hoped this time she wasn't flying too close to the sun.

"Here you go."

The accommodations into which she stepped oozed western bric-a-brac. A picture of a cowboy riding the range hung on the wall with a frame constructed of shiny horseshoes. On a small dresser beneath the artwork sat a lamp with a base carved like a boot and a rawhide shade whipstitched around the edges with a leather thong.

She placed her belongings on the old brass bed. The faded pillowcases were hand embroidered, and a patchwork quilt dipped over the edge to meet the cotton ruffled bed skirt. A comfy chair by the window offered a perfect view. Nearby, the magazine rack, holding copies of hunting, fishing, and horsey oriented periodicals, showcased an adult male's touch. Even so, picturing Hudson staying in the room took a bit of an effort.

"The décor suited me better when I was twelve. My aunt Betty decorated everything long ago, and I haven't had the heart to change much in here."

"It's enchanting. The dream of every little cowboy or cowgirl."

Hudson's gaze traveled around the room. "Toward the end, Uncle Louie acted like he was ready to join Aunt Betty. A consolation, I guess. Do you ever contemplate the afterlife?"

Gees, the conversation sure had taken a turn for the deep and philosophical. She wanted to plop down in the chair and not dwell on anything, let alone a topic this personal. Still, his question offered an opportunity to share data she hadn't recorded or revealed to anyone.

Leaning against the edge of the bed, she plucked at the bedspread with one hand and hedged, not willing to go first. "That's quite the question. What's your take?"

He grinned, as if realizing she'd turned the tables. "When I stand out under the night sky, as we did a few minutes ago, I believe someone greater than us puny humans had a hand in creating such glory. I don't rule out evolution or the abundance of scientific data either. I guess, for me, it's a mash-up of various theories."

His answer pretty much reflected her own conclusions. But her stomach tightened at revealing the tiny bit of information she'd kept secret all this time.

Would he label her a weirdo? She was about to find out. "Generally speaking, I'm of a like mind. However, I saw one more thing with all three of the VR conversions, and you'll be the first person I've told."

His gaze intensified. "Thank you for trusting me. What did you see?"

"At the very end of each recording, and I mean the very end, a light appears."

"You mean the typical go into the light deal?"

"Not exactly. It's more a cluster of sparkles, like fireflies. They hang together and flit around. Not in a panic, but joyfully. Then the tiny orbs break apart, spiral upward, and disappear. Not having any data on the first victim, Alesha Cartwright, I can't know if it would have occurred with her. And originally, I had to consider the phenomenon might be an irregularity in the equipment. But as of Georgia Tarkington's playback today, it's happened with the last three women.

"In all the horror generated by watching these fatal recalls, this tiny bit of brightness is a flash of overwhelming goodness. When I worry about losing my mind because of what I've seen, remembering the intensity of that moment gives me a huge amount of peace. Am I going off the deep end?"

"No. And whether or not you can explain the phenomenon, this is the only uplifting piece of information I've heard since this all began. It's a comforting thought."

"I think so too—at least we have one thing in common."

"Only one?" He seemed serious.

She liked to imagine the strong sexual attraction she'd felt when they'd kissed at the house was a second thing. A big, scary, wonderful second thing.

"I'm sure if we put out heads together, we could come up with several more feelings we've in common." She'd given him the perfect lead in, but he ambled toward the door and didn't seem inclined to explore the obvious.

"Well, it's late, and you've had a big day. Do you need anything—food, a glass of water, a bedtime story?"

A story sounded good. One about how the bad guy got caught and the two of them ended up in each other's arms. Her fantasizing had to be coming from New Brain. "No, I'm good. Thank you. Well, maybe a glass of wine to settle my nerves."

"Sorry, no wine. But Uncle Louie used to stash a bottle of redeye in the kitchen. I'll be right back."

Before she could protest, he was gone. She unpacked what little clothes she'd brought and released her hair from the messy bun at the nape of her neck. She could tell Hudson was interested in her, but maybe more importantly, he didn't seem to have intentions of taking advantage of her staying here. Although feeling a tad rejected, deep down she appreciated his consideration.

Brushing her hair, she stood at the window. Room-light spilled over the windowsill illuminating a scraggly peony bush growing a few inches from the side of the house. Bringing the plant back to good health wouldn't take much effort. Although they were finished blooming for the year, she pondered what color the blossoms would be come next summer.

Hearing the rattle of a teacup on a saucer, she turned to find Hudson standing in the doorway staring at her. He extended the offering. "I diluted a healthy shot of bourbon with chamomile tea. I advise sipping not gulping. It's at least eighty proof."

Tossing the brush on the bed, she reached for the drink and following his advice, tried a small sampling. Heat from the tea and liquor spread throughout her with a welcoming glow. "Thank you. It's perfect." She nodded over her shoulder. "What color are the flowers when the peony is in bloom?"

He made to leave, then paused. "You'll have to come back in the summer and see for yourself."

Chapter Eleven

Despite yesterday's VR session, her house catching on fire, and having spent the night in a strange bed, Marilyn slept like a rock. Maybe the whiskey had something to do with the deep dreamless slumber.

Dragging on sweatpants, a purple Henley, and a hoody, she jammed her feet into socks and sneakers and headed for the bathroom. One of the towels was damp. Hudson was already up.

As she brushed her teeth and washed her face, the enticing aroma of coffee brewing and bacon frying sneaked under the bathroom door tantalizing her senses. She usually didn't eat a big breakfast, but today she was famished.

Hudson stood at the stove cooking. The kitchen table set for two.

"Good morning." She hesitated at the door.

"Good morning to you too. Have a seat."

"Can I help with anything?"

"Nope. Save your strength for barn chores."

Chores? Of course. She supposed helping was fair.

Settling into a chair, she eyed the two well-mannered dogs sitting in their respective doggy beds by the stove. Relying on New Brain data from LeAnn Swanson the dog groomer, she recognized the canines as blue-eyed Australian Shepherds. Being quite large for the breed, and with an extra dash of white hair thrown in, there might be a bit of Great Pyrenees in the mix.

Hudson brought two heaping plates of food to the table. She thanked him for the one he placed in front of her. Before he sat down to feed himself, he reached for two bowls and filled them with kibble. The shepherds leaped up, their mouths aquiver. Short of drooling, they gazed at him with adoring and hopeful expressions.

Marilyn came close to drooling herself as she waited for Hudson to join her at the table. When he did so, she dug into the eggs, toast, and hash browns. He'd left the bacon off her plate, but the aroma nearly had her breaking her vow to not eat meat. "Your dogs are well behaved," she managed between mouthfuls. "What are their names?"

"Frank and Joe Hearty. They look like brothers, so it's my humorous take on the proverbial mystery books which I loved as a kid." He glanced fondly at his two canines as they wolfed down their food. "I got lucky with these guys. When you take in rescues, it's anybody's guess how things will turn out."

"And now you rescued me. Thank you, again." How would things turn out between them?

"You're welcome, Marilyn." He reached for the coffee pot and refilled both their cups.

For the first time, he'd called her Marilyn, not Miss Marilyn or Dr. Monrose—that seemed significant.

"After morning chores," he added, "you can analyze your video on your laptop while I check in again with the DPD. Your tip about the tattoo might have paid off. The bald thing is not very definitive though. A guy could shave his head and face, then grow the hair back changing his appearance relatively quickly."

"Not this guy," she countered. "Last night, I considered what I'd seen. There was no hair at all. No eyebrows, no eyelashes, nothing. He has a condition preventing hair growth. Or maybe he had chemo recently. Not likely I suppose, but a consideration."

Hudson stopped eating, as if mulling over this new information. "That's different and could be useful. You'd make a good PI, doctor."

A fun idea. She supposed working out a scientific equation demanded the same methodical steps as tracking down a killer. Either way, you needed as many parts to the puzzle as possible.

A raucous noise outside shattered the silence. She glanced up in surprise.

"That's Hank, my donkey. He alerts me when breakfast in the barn is running late."

"He's a good spokesperson. I don't doubt his bray can be heard for miles. You have quite the collection of critters here."

"Indeed, I do."

Indulging in another leisurely moment, they each finished off another half cup of coffee. Then together they cleared the table and put the dishes to soak.

"Wait until you meet the goats. They love company. Come on, boys, let's show Marilyn around outside." Tails wagging, Frank and Joe Hearty jumped at the chance.

****

Hud was pleased by Marilyn's enthusiasm for the out of doors. Even wearing designer sneakers, she tackled the terrain well, navigating around the largest of the puddles.

"What can I do to help?"

After he turned the horse and donkey out to graze, he scooped a cup of chow into two separate tin pans and handed them off to her. "These are for the goats, Jessabelle and Jubilee. When you enter their pen, they may try and latch onto your hoodie or any handy piece of clothing. They're not trying to bite you. They were taken from their mom too soon and like sucking on the material like a pacifier. I'll be right behind you with the hay."

She unlatched the gate and went in first. The two Nubians ran toward her. Unafraid, she held her ground and the pans on high. "Good morning, ladies. Yes, I have your kibble. Now behave yourselves. Here's one for you. Easy now. And one over here for you." She set down the pans several feet apart. As the Nubians ate peacefully, she stroked one of the goat's soft floppy ears.

"What's your secret? They never listen to me like that. They usually fuss with one another when eating." He placed the hay he carried in their big rubber tub.

"I'm the goat whisperer. Remember, I told you about my uncle's farm in Michigan, and the goats. I've always had a way with them, and these two pretty gals are darling."

"If you say so. They aren't so polite when I try to wrestle their coats on in the winter."

"Call me, and I'll lend a hand."

"That sounds promising." He stepped closer, encircling her waist with his arms. What a perfect way to start the morning—a beautiful woman in his arms, the scent of fresh hay all around, the animals fed and as content as he felt right now.

When his ex stayed here, she never left the house. Calling the animals smelly, making him change clothes and shower before even holding her hand. The signs had been obvious, but hope had sprung—if not eternal, at least for a little while.

Marilyn leaned closer. Reproaching himself for thinking about someone else, he dipped his head to steal a kiss. She kissed him back, and the desire to have his way with her right now had him wanting more. When she slipped her hands inside his jacket, he grabbed her backside and drew her hips indecently close. At the sudden contact, they both uttered a sound of pleasure.

"I've wanted you from the first time I saw you at your lab."

"You caught my eye too. But you were rather intimidating."

"I don't think either one of us were in a good place that day."

"We're not in a much better place now regarding the murders."

"No, but at least we're facing things together."

One of the goats gave Marilyn a head-butt to the thigh, knocking her sideways.

"Hey, settle down." Hud stepped between Marilyn and the rowdy Nubian. "I believe she's jealous. We had better vacate their territory before they gang up on us."

"Or before we do something we might regret"

"Regret was the farthest thing from my mind." But the interruption was timely. He needed to get out of here and cool down. He intended for his relationship with Marilyn to be more than a quick roll in the hay—literally and figuratively.

Leading her from the goat pen, he secured both

locks.

"Why two?"

"Goats spend half the day eating and half the day figuring how to get out of whatever you put them in. They're smart and persistent and rarely fail to make me a laugh. Unless they do get out. Then they're the only ones who find the situation amusing."

Frank and Joe Hearty waited in the center aisle of the barn, tongues lolling and ready to go. Hud pushed the wheelbarrow toward the horse and donkey stalls, the dogs following on his heels. "What is my lady's preference, shovel or manure fork?"

She grabbed the fork.

"Wise choice."

****

An hour later, Marilyn walking at his side, Hud headed back to the house.

"Country living is more fun than I imagined."

"Be still my heart. You actually think this is fun?"

"Well, I'm not on duty every day. I'm sure it gets old, especially in the winter when the snow is two feet deep."

"Sometimes three feet. But if there's enough food to go around, snowbound can be pretty fun too—when you're with someone special."

"Am I special, Hudson?"

The question took him off guard, but his answer came quickly. "Definitely."

"No one's said anything like that to me in an awfully long time."

"Stick around. I'll make sure you hear those words more often."

"A tempting offer." Her noncommittal response

left possibilities to be explored and his attitude optimistic.

They entered the house via the mudroom and washed up, then he showed her his office, a small offshoot of the main living area. She took the chair by the bookshelf and fired up her laptop.

"Will you be all right going through all this on your own?"

"Yes. I should be fine. This flash drive contains my reaction to the reintegrated EEG, not the images projected in my mind. Reviewing the footage helps me determine if changes are in order, such as the placement of the chair or how the room is set up. Stuff like that."

"Sounds good. I'm going to check in with the DPD." Stepping out of the room so they could both have privacy, he brought up Marco's name on his cell phone and punched enter. His friend answered on the second ring.

"Hey, man, I heard through the grapevine about the house fire at Dr. Monrose's." There was concern in Marco's voice. "They said you were okay, are you?"

"Yes. We're both fine. She's with me now at the farm."

"Is that a smart move, buddy?" Concern still edged Marco's tone, but on a different level. "Much as I'd love to know you have a new lady in your life, you shouldn't be involved with a person so closely connected to the case."

"I wouldn't exactly say we're involved. She needed a place to stay, end of story."

"Uh huh. Keep in mind she could have set the fire herself. Which, by the way, forensics has confirmed it to be arson. A slow burn, started in the basement."

"Now why would she do that?"

"Why not? Your last girlfriend keyed your truck and punctured two tires when she left. You attract abandoned animals and crazy women."

"Now don't start talkin' trash about my animals. Besides, you couldn't even manage to take care of one cockapoo. Last year when the woman you broke up with left, she took the dog too, and you were glad to have them both gone."

"What are you talking about? You got that all wrong. She moved across the country for a new job, and the dog was to remind her of me."

"You're a far cry from a cockapoo, and Utah is hardly across the country. You didn't even try to keep in touch or get the dog back."

"Long distance never works. I'm a hands on kinda guy, if you get my drift. Anyway, she was getting overly serious, and the dog did nothing but bark. Besides, you're the one who enjoys a steady relationship, of which you have none."

"Don't start." How had Marco managed to circle back around to his love life? He needed to change the subject pronto. "Any luck tracking down Warren Jameson?"

"No. But we obtained a warrant and searched his apartment. He's in the wind. Left in a hurry and didn't leave any useful intel behind as to where he might be."

"Interesting. How about suspects from the tattoo rendering?"

"It's still in the computation phase. A nationwide search takes a while. If we don't turn up anything there, we can go global. Although I get the feeling our boy's local. I've also been promised an updated list of recent releases from the mental facilities still in operation. We need a whole lot more of those places."

"Boy do we ever. Although some were horror shows, shutting down those facilities in the seventies and eighties bordered on cruelty, leaving untold numbers of people with nowhere to go."

"I agree. And it's no better now. Thousands of people are out there abandoned and ignored, living on the fringe of society. And now too many vets have joined the ranks. How they're treated is shameful. Some of those old places needed to go, but not all of them."

"While we're searching knee deep in this misery, keep all the privacy and human rights regulations in mind," Hud cautioned. "Any misstep to get evidence could be used against the case."

"Yeah, yeah. Much as I want to get my hands on this miserable misfit, I'll play by the book. I wish you would have done the same, but I respect why you didn't."

"I appreciate you saying so, Marco. That means a lot coming from one of the best cops I've ever known. I didn't feel I had a choice."

"I know. Now knock it off. You're gonna make me blush. I'll relay any new data to you regarding the suspects."

"Great. And by the way. Dr. Monrose said the killer might have a medical condition preventing hair growth. Maybe genetic. The theory sounds worth checking out, will you pass along the idea."

"You got it. Have fun playing doctor."

The connection went dead before Hud could fire back a smart response.

****

Marilyn viewed and then stored the flash drive with the other Georgia Tarkington information.

She hadn't grown accustomed to watching herself crawl around, gain her feet, crash into walls, and then drop to the floor and go still—as if dead. No wonder for days following an experiment she felt like she'd been hit by a truck.

This time, flashes of Hudson could be seen in the footage. Once or twice, he'd reached out as if to help. Then, true to his word, he caught himself and backed off. All except one time when she'd been barreling toward the edge of the alcove, he stepped in front of her so she bounced off his chest rather than the corner of the doorway.

She was really beginning to like this man, an unexpected phenomenon in the middle of this unprecedented situation. He seemed to trust her more. Enough to share info with her from his friend Marco and the DPD.

And then there was the sexual chemistry developing between them, ready to synthesize and combust. She hadn't felt this kind of first-time crush exuberance since she was in high school. Heart palpitationy and girlish, she wanted to scrawl his name over and over in different style penmanship in her notebook. The thought had her stepping back in time to when she first experienced the throes of love in its purest form. Old Brain or New Brain? Frankly, she didn't care.

As if her daydreaming had drawn him near, Hudson appeared at the open door. "How are things going?"

"Doing okay."

"Your face is flushed."

She pressed her hands to her cheeks. They did feel hot. "Just a reaction from wrestling with some overwhelming thoughts"

Squeezing past her in the limited space, Hudson dropped down onto the seat in front of the computer. "Marco says they're working on the tattoo angle."

"Good. Let's hope the idea pans out. I made a list of conditions often leading to hair loss. Genetic causes are quite rare, so if they were studied and published in JAMA or a similar medical journal, we might have access to a patient name or the physician who treated him. On the downside, people can react with hair loss from nutritional deficiencies or even common medications a primary care physician would prescribe. You know, like antidepressants, cholesterol-lowering drugs, beta-blockers. Our killer could be one of millions."

"What are the genetic or immunological conditions? You said totally devoid of hair so that sounds pretty serious and more of a possibility."

"Alopecia, lupus, Hashimoto's disease, Graves' disease, congenital hypotrichosis, and congenital atrichia."

"Please tell me you've written those names down, because I can't spell ninety-nine percent of what you said."

"You can make a printout from this." She handed him a flash drive which he plugged into his computer.

"If you plan on going to Denver, we could stop by the lab and crosscheck the info online. I have more clearance for medical journals on that computer."

"Sure, sounds good. We can also swing by the

DPD and touch base with Marco in person."

"Are you okay with me staying at your place a little longer?"

"Better than okay. You're welcome here as long as you want. You haven't even seen the hot tub yet. Or the potting shed."

"You have a hot tub? Somehow I can't picture that."

"Actually, it's a stock tank using rainwater and a solar heater."

"How Rube Goldberg of you."

He gave a sheepish smile. "Not high-tech, but it still feels mighty good on a cold autumn evening."

A warm soak sounded just the thing for her aching body and stressed out mind.

"What's so special about the potting shed?"

"Blatantly Victorian, with glass panels and wrought iron doodads, the structure has stood there for quite some time, and it's fun to look at and poke around in."

"How intriguing. I would definitely like a tour sometime. And thank you for extending my visit for gosh knows how long." Did she dare impose on his good humor a little more? "Since I'm begging favors, while we're in town, can we run by my house so I can pick up more clean clothes?"

"Sure. Whatever you want."

"I also want to doublecheck for any data I may have accidently left behind. I've paid for that research with blood, sweat, and fear. No way I'm losing one tortured paragraph. Once I'm sure I have it all, I can transfer everything to a lock box or something. Right now, I'm not sure who to trust."

"I hope you know you can trust me."

"I want to, Hudson."

"Good. Then let's hit the road. The DPD first, then your house, and then your lab."

****

Their stop at the DPD had been brief and offered no new clues regarding the investigation.

Visiting her house was less routine and more emotional. Her home appeared sad. The safety inspection had yet to be finished, but nothing would prevent Marilyn from going inside. Her determination must have shown on her face because Hudson didn't try to stop her.

He did insist, however, going in with her, and while he busied himself fixing the loose board on the stairs, she started gathering essentials.

The idea of using a suitcase crossed her mind, but she feared the image would freak Hudson out giving the impression she was moving in forever. Instead, she unearthed a rucksack from her college days and stuffed it to the gills, including the new more serviceable footwear she'd purchased.

"We should probably get going," Hudson warned.

Knowing safety could be an issue, she located and grabbed a few papers that had slid under the rolltop desk and was ready to leave.

At the Kingsley Institute, they lucked out and found a parking space out front.

Reaching her work area, she logged into her server and began researching the diseases they considered pertinent. Hudson sat nearby using her backup computer. Having another person working in her lab felt weird, demanding extra effort to keep her mind focused on the man they searched for rather than the man at her side.

While at the DPD, she'd met Marco, a person Hudson apparently held in high esteem. The introduction started off strained, and the detective had bluntly asked about her staying at Hudson's house. Marco's protective attitude spoke of the deep friendship and the high opinion the two men held for one another. She wished she had a friend as loyal as Marco.

After she'd offered free access to all her pertinent information and admitted to enjoying the country atmosphere at the farm, Marco seemed to relax. By the time they were ready to depart, he'd procured temporary authorization for Marilyn to officially collaborate with Hudson and the DPD. A bittersweet honor considering the horrific reason.

Her auxiliary computer beeped, bringing her back to the matter at hand.

"Hey," Hudson gave a heads up. "The files Marco promised are coming in. Looks like there are five persons of interest considered likely suspects from the two lists we're working with.

"Three of them have been recently released from prison, and two are from mental facilities. Here are the names and a meager bit of background on each one."

Marilyn gained her feet and went to stand beside the computer. Resisting the urge to touch Hudson's shoulder, she clenched her hands behind her back and leaned over him for a better view. He smelled fresh and clean like the hay he fed his animals and the great outdoors he seemed to favor. The combination was as captivating as any aftershave or cologne on the market.

He glanced up and caught her gazing at him instead

of the screen. She straightened and asked if there were any file photos. Rather than give her a hard time, he cut her a break and brought up the images.

"These are the three from the federal judicial system. Tattoos are noted as affirmative on all of them, but the descriptions don't match the one you saw. Of course, your particular tattoo could have been added after their release. This one is a hairy son of a gun, so I say he's out. Two are skin heads, so they're a partial fit, but both have eyebrow and lip piercings."

"And the two from the mental facilities?"

"The details are sketchier for them. Due to the HIPAA laws there are roadblocks on digging deeper."

"The photos aren't very good either," she noted. "But the one with the hat—there's something striking about his eyes." The name beneath the picture read Archibald Underwood. "The hate emanating from them is terrifyingly familiar." Forcing herself not to turn away, she trembled and felt woozy.

Hudson was on his feet in a flash. "Here." He pushed her onto the seat he'd vacated. "Your face is white as fresh snow."

She felt nearly as cold.

He rolled the other office chair over beside her and sat down. "Does he look familiar?"

"I can't say for sure." She gave another shiver.

"Let's catch our breath, then we can grab lunch in town and continue with this when we get home. I mean when we get back to my place."

At the word home, a bit of warmth seeped into her bones.

Chapter Twelve

Archie picked up the transistor radio he'd spent the last of his money on and tuned in the news station. The signal was poor and bled over into a nearby channel playing heavy metal music. He could barely concentrate on the news announcer's words over the pounding beat and screaming voices. His mind often felt tuned into two stations—especially since he hadn't taken his meds in weeks.

He finally gave up and switched off the radio. Her voice immediately overtook everything else in his head. Each time he had made sure she was good and dead, yet she kept coming back.

Evil rising, again and again, like a hideous white phoenix.

****

Deciding to remove the most important pieces of her equipment, Marilyn and Hudson now labored their way to the front entry/exit of Kingsley.

Oh dear. She'd forgotten to take off her lab coat. Out of habit, upon arrival she'd shrugged into the white jacket. No matter, she could ditch the coat in Hudson's truck before they got to the restaurant.

They pushed through the double front doors. Flash bulbs went off in their faces, and people gathered out front began shouting questions. "There she is. Dr. Monrose, is it true you're working with the Denver

Police Department?"

Confused, Marilyn's steps faltered. Hudson bullied a path through the crowd of brazen media hounds. She stuck close, nearly tripping them both.

"Can you identify the serial killer? Who is he?" People kept asking one question after another, not waiting for answers.

Making a lumbering dash for Hudson's vehicle, the two of them dropped off the heavy items in the truck bed, then they both jumped in the cab and slammed the doors shut.

In hot pursuit, a tsunami of correspondents flooded across the street behind them. Hudson started the engine and, showing minimal regard for the predatory film crews and reporters, he drove off.

"It can't be." He fishtailed into the street and kept going.

"What do you mean? What's going on?"

"First of all, someone—most likely Warren or whomever he sold the info to—leaked the information regarding your research and the fact you're working with the police on the serial killer case. Secondly, I saw my ex-girlfriend's car. She fancies herself a reporter and works for an on-line magazine called The Low Down in LoDo. No doubt she was among the crowd of news sharks back there."

Before he could add more, Hudson's phone rang. "Hey, Marco. What's up?" There was a pause as he listened, she couldn't hear what was being said. "We're on our way." He returned the phone to his pocket. "They need us back at the DPD."

"Please, please tell me they did not find another body."

"No. There's no new victim. For reasons unknown, Captain Bradshaw wants to talk to the both of us."

Yikes, meeting with and possibly being grilled by the man who ran the homicide department didn't sound so good either. For assorted reasons, she'd been trying to keep a low profile in all this—a valiant attempt apparently blown sky high.

She stared out the window, not taking note of the passing view. When this hit the papers and the institute found out, she'd be in deep doodoo. Slipping her hand into the pocket of her lab coat, she held on tight to the two flash drives she'd brought along. At least most of her equipment was safe, rattling around in the back of the truck with her duffle bag of clothes. Now they couldn't confiscate her equipment.

****

Hud hadn't seen his old boss this angry in quite a long time. "Really, Captain. The first we knew about the press being involved was like two minutes ago when they waylaid us outside the Kingsley Institute."

"I've been getting calls since sunup. And the mayor and the governor have too."

"We're guessing an associate of Dr. Monrose's spilled the information. His name is Warren Jameson, and there's already a BOLO out on him.

"He broke into her house and threatened her with a gun. We're also looking at him for a possible arson attempt, with intent to kill. The leak's not her fault, sir. She's been a big help to the department." Would his soliloquy gain Marilyn at least a little sympathy?

The captain's hardnosed expression did relax a smidgeon. "Yes, we're following up on the Jameson connection to the fire and the leak. We haven't located him or his car, but both are on the priority list. I'm sorry about your troubles, Dr. Monrose. It's my own fault for letting two outsiders in on the case."

The term outsider hit Hud hard. Being labeled as such was his fault and his choice, and he usually didn't regret the decision. "Again, sir, she's contributed some valuable leads. We both have."

"Yes, I'm aware, but at the price of this media circus now busting loose around us. And let the lady speak for herself. She's obviously quite capable. Do you wish to continue being part of the task force trying to catch this serial killer?"

Shoulders squared, chin up, Marilyn stared his ex-boss in the eyes. "Yes, sir. If you'd seen what I have, you'd realize I must do whatever is necessary to stop him."

Hud felt a swell of pride for Marilyn's courage. She could have easily begged off. Especially now since she was probably in trouble at work.

"All right. You both stay—for now. We'll deal with the press as best we can with an official statement later today. Marco will share whatever we come up with, and you two are to do the same—capisce?"

"Yes, Captain, we get it. You'll have our full cooperation. And thank you. We both want to see this through to the end."

"All right. Get out of here."

Like truant grade schoolers fleeing the principal's office, they bumped into one another as they vacated their chairs and exited out the door. Marco was waiting.

"In trouble again, Kincaid?"

"Nothing new there. But we're still both in."

"Good. We're glad for the help. None of us are

going to get any sleep until this guy is behind bars or below the horizon."

"Marilyn, err, Dr. Monrose had a hunch on one of the suspects you e-mailed me earlier."

"Great. Which one?" Marco led the way to a white board standing off to the side of the squad room.

Plastered with photos, maps, diagrams, and handwritten info, the data was laid out rather freeform—until you came to the victims. The file photos of the female faces were displayed precisely and prominently across the top. On the second row were the cringeworthy crime scene shots of the same women. The images of the possible suspects were off to the side as if no one wanted them too close to the women.

Marilyn hung back a second, then stepped up and pointed. "Him." The single word vibrated with absolute loathing. And although her hand shook, her voice was strong and clear. "He's the one." Marilyn again identified Archibald Underwood. This image captured the man's animalistic stare and revealed his completely bald head.

Marco nodded. "We've been leaning toward him as well. Most of the other suspects have, if not airtight, potentially acceptable alibies."

"And this guy?" Hud asked.

"We know who he is, but not where he is."

"What do you mean? How can you not know where he is?"

Grabbing a file from the top of the pile on his desk, Marco flipped open the folder. "Arrested in 1989 for murder, he was declared criminally insane at trial and taken to a maximum-security mental health detention center. He underwent years of therapy while being pumped full of every old and new psychiatric drug available.

"Finally deemed manageable and no longer a threat to others, they relocated him from a high-level security facility to a general population mental hospital in eastern Colorado—from where he recently escaped."

"Escaped? When? How?"

"From an outdated sanitarium, located ironically in a town named Happy Valley. Due to faulty wiring, an electrical fire broke out in the laundry area, and three patients escaped. Two were found wandering around, but not the third. Our murders started two weeks later. The MO Underwood used in the original murder for which he was convicted matches the MO used in the current homicides."

Finally, they were making progress. "Who was his first victim?"

"His mother."

A moment or two passed before Hud could wrap his mind around what he'd heard, and from the blank stare on Marilyn's face she was having the same reaction. This was the depths of depravation. "How could he do these things to any human being, let alone his own mother?"

"That's what we're trying find out, but there's a bale of red tape to cut through before we get the medical records—or even his trial transcripts. We're pulling out all the stops and pulling in all the favors."

"Does he have a tattoo?" Marilyn asked.

"We aren't sure, nothing registered. His doctor at Happy Valley would know, but we're waiting for permission to speak with him. Meanwhile we're keeping up the organized searches fanning out from the murder scenes."

"At least we have a most-likely suspect. A huge leap from where we were. With a name, maybe we can tie him back to one of the victims or figure out the reason behind the attacks. The info won't make any difference to the current victims but might help stop this psycho from killing someone else."

"I'll keep you in the loop," Marco promised.

Hud nodded. "We'll do follow-up research from my place."

Chapter Thirteen

Sneaking out the back way, Marilyn and Hudson avoided the press lying in wait at the DPD's front door. After picking up another allotment of groceries, they reached the farm by late afternoon.

Still bruised and sore from yesterday's VR session, Marilyn allowed herself to be sweettalked into using the *hot tub.*

The solar heated water was deliciously warm, and the idea turned out to be a good one. But she hadn't brought a swimsuit and, no matter how tempting, knew she shouldn't go commando. Settling on a T-shirt and panties, a large fluffy beach towel waited nearby for her to use as a cover-up when she got out.

Not far from the house, the small metal stock tank sat surrounded by a wooden trellis bearing honeysuckle vines. With the last blooms of the season giving off a heady perfume, the countrified picture was complete.

Drowsy, she floated, consciously blocking the terrifying recollections she'd seen. And the fact her house was a crispy critter. And how Warren—whom she'd considered a friend—had viciously turned on her. All the chaos and horror would be there an hour from now. This was her time—much needed and appreciated.

A sensuous languor overtook her, sending her musings drifting back to Hudson. A twenty-first century lawman-cowboy, he seemed to have old-fashioned values, yet enough bad boy in him to break the rules when needed. And she'd seen firsthand how he treated his animals with kindness and patience, always a good sign.

Living in the same house as Hudson, taking things slowly became a hard vow to honor. Grazing her hand across the front of her body, she wasn't sure she'd be able to hold out much longer.

During college and graduate school, she'd had neither the time nor inclination for a full-blown relationship. More free-spirited back then, an occasional slam, bam, thank you ma'am, had worked for her. Then, while fighting her way to the top of a field mostly dominated by men, she successfully kept things professional at work until Warren, her first slipup—a costly one.

She slid lower in the water, waves lapping at her chin. There she went again, worrying about past mistakes and current complications. Hadn't she decided to give herself a break? Switching off the thoughts rambling around in her brain, she gazed out over the prairie. As the evening approached, shadows artistically fell into place, and the earthy floral fragrances swirling around calmed her spirit.

Remembering the wine, she made a monumental effort to scoot upright and reached over the side feeling around for the plastic glass. The dark merlot they'd purchased in town hit the spot. Issuing a huge sigh, she leaned her head back on the top ridge of the tank. Perfect. Now she was in the zone.

What the heck.

She felt a tug on the scrunchie keeping her hair in place. Had Hudson sneaked up on her to play a silly schoolboy prank?

"What are you doing?"

The second tug was more insistent.

"Ouch." This time his shenanigans hurt as the tie tore loose setting her hair free.

She placed the wine glass back on the ground and shifting around came face to face with Jessabelle and Jubilee. The goats, merely inches away, stared at her with their weird golden eyes. Jubilee held the scrunchie in her mouth.

"Don't you dare eat that." Marilyn knew goats enjoyed a wide variety of plants, but she doubted rubber and polyester fabric would do the animal's digestion any good—no matter how many stomachs were involved.

Jubilee seemed to consider the stern request. Jessabelle stuck her head in the tub and began sucking up water.

Easing upright, Marilyn gained her feet and grabbed for the hair tie. As if to taunt her, both goats stepped back in unison, precisely out of arm's reach.

She shoved her hair out of her eyes, stepped over the side of the tank, and wedged her feet into waiting sandals. "Nice goatie. Give me the hair tie."

Twisting off a branch of honeysuckle, she offered the tidbit in trade. The scheme went ignored. Droplets of water still clinging to Jessabelle's muzzle, she gave an astonishingly loud sneeze. At the unexpected noise, Marilyn dropped the branch. As if on cue, Jubilee dropped the scrunchie.

Marilyn bent to snag the hair tie just as Frank and Joe Hearty came loping around the edge of the trees. The great escape had been discovered. The two goats, knowing they'd been caught, turned to run. Clambering about, they knocked into her, and with a yelp of surprise Marilyn hit the slippery water-soaked ground. All four animals thundered off toward the barn.

"What's going on out here? I heard the dogs barking." Hudson stopped short, then hurried forward. "You okay?" Reaching down he gave her a hand up. "You certainly win the wet T-shirt contest."

Marilyn glanced at the nearly transparent material. "Yikes." Grabbing the towel, she held it to her chest. Hudson shrugged out of his flannel shirt and draped the soft warm fabric across her shoulders.

With the initial hubbub over, the dogs expertly herded the goats along in the right direction.

"Can you make your way back to the house on your own? I had better go lock up the girls."

She raked one hand through her bedraggled wet hair. "Yes, I'm fine. Go round up your wayward children." She could hardly wait for him to leave. She must look a mess…again.

Brushing off the dirt and leaves stuck to her backside and traveling as fast as her sandals would allow in the treacherous terrain, she escaped to the house.

****

While Hudson secured his two errant ladies, Marilyn cleaned up and shimmied into a dark green fleecy dress. Long and cozy, and tight in all the right places, the incredibly soft material showed off her curves without being obvious. If more people wore clothes made from this dreamy fabric, the world would be a better place.

Hudson had previously started a fire in the

woodstove, which was nearly out. She stirred the coals and added kindling and two small logs. The flames quickly took hold, leaping up to warm the kettle of water on top.

Raiding the new stock of supplies, she fixed two salads and placed them in the fridge for later. When the kettle on the woodstove hissed and spit, she made a cup of tea and curled up in one of the big, overstuffed chairs. All this peace and quiet couldn't have come at a better time in her life.

For Marilyn, the future had always taken a backseat to the here and now. She'd been conscientious enough to make plans for her financial security, such as a 401-K and a Roth IRA plan, but she'd taken no steps toward securing any type of emotional wellbeing. Gad, she was starting to sound OLD. And she was beginning to feel way too comfortable here.

Hudson returned, carrying another armload of wood which he stacked near the stove. Turning, he dusted the wood flakes from his hands as he studied her.

"All critters present and accounted for. I did the evening chores too, so we're in for the night. Which is probably a good thing because the clouds building off to the west could bring a dusting of snow by morning."

She'd forgotten about feeding the animals. "I'm sorry, I should have helped you in the barn."

"Not your animals, not your problem, but thanks. Besides you make quite the picture, curled up there like a contented kitten. Nice finding you waiting by the woodstove."

"I'm totally relaxed. And the hot tub felt great. But now all I can think about is food."

"Me too. I already started the grill on the deck."

While Hudson barbecued a steak for him and a gorgeous plump portabella mushroom for her, Marilyn set the table, and got out the side salads. Then she went old style and heated up a can of German potato salad.

****

Dinner over and the dishes done, they sat in front of the woodstove nibbling on the brownies Hudson insisted on buying in the bakery department.

Another indulgence, and the breaking of more rules. If she stayed here much longer, she'd need to plot a running track on the property.

Although he'd appeared totally relaxed, when Hudson's computer signaled an incoming message, he launched himself out of his chair to check the screen in his office. She was right behind him.

"Wow. The DPD got a court order for medical records relating to our prime suspect. They're transmitting the info now." He typed in a reply, backed up the file, and started printing.

Handing off several of the papers spewing forth, he kept half the pages for himself. When there weren't any more, they both sat down in front of the stove to read.

Hudson broke the silence. "Holy cow, listen to this. He's been institutionalized since the age of thirteen, the age when he killed his mother. According to the police report, when she failed to show up for work at the beauty shop, they made a safety check and found her body in the basement of the family home."

"Good grief. I can't even imagine what goes on inside a mind like that." To explore, in great detail, the neurological, physiological, and psychological aspects of Archibald Underwood would be a fascinating and horrifying undertaking.

Flipping through the pages, she searched for a diagnosis and a list of what treatments he may have been given.

"Here." She stabbed a finger at a specific line in the document. "Schizoaffective disorder. The diagnosis has been mentioned more than once."

"What exactly are we talking about here?"

"It's when a patient has the symptoms of both schizophrenia and a mood disorder such as depression, or a bipolar condition."

"That doesn't sound good."

"No. It isn't. A living hell most likely. The list of meds he's supposed to be on, and has taken at one time or another, is shocking and long. They tried everything, old remedies, herbal remedies, experimental remedies, and all the latest antipsychotics. They even gave him hydro-shock and electroshock treatments. The only thing they left out was a lobotomy."

"Too bad."

Hudson's statement left her at a loss for words. If they'd performed the archaic monstrous procedure, would four young women be alive?

"After all those years, what do you suppose set him off leading to his escape?" Hudson levered to his feet and stood waiting for her answer.

"Maybe an inciting incident, or simply because the opportunity presented itself in the laundry area. Here's another concern. Since he went AWOL, he's quit cold turkey all the meds he was on recently. He's a walking madhouse."

Hudson shoved another log into the woodstove and

settled back into his chair. "It says here when he was upgraded and moved from a criminally insane state-run hospital to a maximum-security mental institution, he worked in the laundry where the fire started. Was he cognizant of his surroundings and smart enough to start the fire, engineering the escape?"

"Absolutely. After all the drugs and shock therapy, you wouldn't suspect there'd be any gray matter left with which to work. Yet according to his test scores he's quite intelligent. Which makes him all the more dangerous. He's living in his own world—slipping back into ours often enough to get by on the streets and follow through with his compulsions. He's obsessed by something we can't see or imagine, and he won't stop."

"We need more personal information rather than charts and test scores. You know, his likes and dislikes. While he was institutionalized, what did he read, what did he talk about? A glimpse as to how he thinks—if that's at all possible."

"There's a phone number listed for his physician at the institution. Speaking to him doctor to doctor might prove illuminating."

They both glanced at the clock on the shelf. Wow, 10 P.M. already.

"Probably to our advantage to wait and try him in the morning." She set the page with the phone number off to one side.

"I agree. Clearing the call with the captain first is a must too."

Hudson closed the damper on the woodstove and stretched. "On that note, I'm for bed. We'll need to be up early to do chores and make the morning briefing Marco texted me about. He's off the second shift and back on days. It's all hands on deck until this is over."

"Okay. Sounds good. See you in the morning. I'll get the light." She stood and hugged herself wishing Hudson's arms were wrapped around her and keeping her warm.

"Good night, Marilyn."

"Good night, Hudson."

After he left, she wandered over to the woodstove and reveled in the last of the heat radiating off the cast iron. Hudson assumed they would sleep in separate beds again tonight—both a noble and disappointing proposition.

Chapter Fourteen

Early the next morning, Archie poked around the nearby trash bin and retrieved a rumpled copy of the Denver Post. Annoyed by the sunlight, he hurried back to the safety of his refuge. Flopping into a chair that had seen better days, he read about his missions and chuckled at the daily cartoons.

Another article caught his attention. The story indicated a Dr Marilyn Monrose knew what he looked like, and she was working with the police.

How could this be? No one ever noticed him by the light of day, and he was as elusive as black cat in the dead of night. He stared at the basement wall, it began to shimmer and move. He heard footsteps. Was she coming? The wall transformed again. There was the table and chairs from his childhood, his shelf of books, and Princess his cat. He reached for the beloved animal. She disappeared. Then he remembered she was dead. They were all dead, just illusions meant to taunt him. He squeezed his eyes shut tight. Blackness was better than the twisted visions.

He began to sweat and shake, breathing too rapidly. Nausea roiled in his belly, and he feared he might throw up. For the first time, he wished he had the pills they forced him to take at the sanitarium. The blue ones stopped his heart from racing and beating off-rhythm. The pound of flesh vibrated harder, erratically, as if intending to jump out of his chest.

Daring to look again his gaze fell on the newspaper. The photo with the disturbing article showed a man and woman as they left a big brick building. She was wearing a white coat.

As if punched in the head, the buzzing in his brain erupted with such force he nearly tumbled from his chair. “Stay away. How many will be enough?”

Grabbing the toy tiger, he stroked the damaged fur, and rocking back and forth he howled like a wounded animal.

****

The police department morning meeting was about to begin, and those present gathered in a rarely used backroom. The windows were few, with dust buildup in the corners. A dismal atmosphere for their dismal situation.

Marilyn took a seat across from Hudson. Sitting beside him seemed obvious and cutesy, and she needed to stand on her own in this group if she was going to be taken seriously and gain any credibility.

Captain Bradshaw was overseeing the briefing. “By now you should all have read the medical documents released last night regarding our suspect.” Murmurs and nods of assent rippled through the group. “I’m here to give you my eyewitness account of the police call and the questioning when our suspect was first arrested those many years ago.”

“You can’t be that old,” Marco piped up. Now a wave of poorly concealed laughter swept the room.

“I was a rookie at the time, Moretti. Pay attention.”

“Yes, sir. I meant you look so young. How can it be?”

"Right. Well, this case is aging me fast. Now listen up. As stated in the report, the DPD originally entered the house in response to a wellness check request. The mother of our suspect worked at a hair salon doing nails mostly. Supposedly the husband had run off three years before, leaving her on her own with one son to raise—Archibald. He was often truant at school and complained of being bullied and ridiculed. His mother began homeschooling him, or so she claimed. Other than a large collection of worn paperback books in the basement, there wasn't much evidence of an educational program taking place.

"When we entered the premises, the smell was overwhelming. We found the mother's body sitting at a table in the basement. She wore her white smock from work, and her severed right hand lay beside her on the tabletop. During the scene investigation, we found another body in the basement. This one appeared to have been buried approximately two or three years earlier. Later, the remains were identified as Archibald's father. Also present was a dead cat, ceremonially displayed on a makeshift altar."

The captain paused, giving everyone time to digest what he'd revealed.

"Rotten food, empty cans and bottles, a bucket with traces of human urine and feces led us to believe someone, at least on occasion, inhabited the cellar. The basement door had a slide bolt on the outside with no means of opening the lock from within."

"Did he confess to both murders?" Hudson asked.

"No, just the mother's. He said she killed the father and made him help to bury the body. After that, while she entertained her gentleman callers, she locked him in the basement—his dead father and a cat his only companions."

"Did he get bullied in school due to his lack of hair?" All eyes turned toward Marilyn. But not to worry, she'd come prepared.

"The record shows they called him names and beat him up, but an exact motive for the cruelty isn't listed. It's possible that's the reason they picked on him. What are the details, Dr. Monrose?"

"His record indicates he has a true case of congenital hypotrichosis. In other words, no hair growth—anywhere. And unlike alopecia, where hair may have formerly existed and then been lost, this is a situation where there wasn't any hair growth in the first place, usually from birth.

"The condition is sometimes accompanied by other physical or mental shortcomings. You can imagine the effect this would have on a child, especially if his mother rejected him. On top of his diagnosis of schizophrenia, his record shows various types of psychosis, with occasions of total reality breaks and madness."

"So, what," Marco cut in heatedly. "He's not a kid anymore. Are we supposed to feel sorry for him because he had a bad childhood?"

"No, of course not. I wasn't making excuses. But how he got this way might give us a hint on how his mind works today, and possibly where he's holed up."

Captain Bradshaw held up a hand to calm the waters. "Thank you, doctor. We will certainly explore those avenues, and we appreciate your input. As far as when our suspect was first arrested, I mostly saw his interview through a two-way mirror.

"He was thirteen but, hunched over and with no hair, you could mistake him for a frail old man, making you doubt how he could have done such a thing—until you saw his eyes. They were piercing, like he saw things you couldn't see. And they were filled with, not hate exactly, but death.

"He told the investigators he always painted the nails on his mother's right hand so they would appear flawless, an example for her customers. Anything less than perfection resulted in a beating and his being locked in the basement whether she had company or not. Asked if that was why he cut off her hand he said no. After stabbing her in her cruel heart, he cut it off because she had used the hand to strangle his cat which had scratched her arm.

"Ruled mentally unredeemable, he was sent to a maximum lockdown facility for the criminally insane. I doubt the conditions there helped, if indeed there was any help to be had for him. After so many years of good behavior, his status was upgraded, and he went to a less formidable, and supposedly more progressive mental institution. From where he escaped."

"We know most of this, how does it help?" Marco persisted.

"Any ideas, Dr. Monrose?"

"He appears to be repeating his original crime over and over, indicating he sees his mother in these women. And being schizophrenic, and most likely paranoid, he believes she is returning over and over to haunt and punish him. His affection for the cat, and the way he reacted to its death, shows an attachment he never found with anyone or anything else.

"Since the basement was a place of refuge as well

as punishment, he would seek similar surroundings now. He's focused on only two things, survival and stopping what he perceives to be his mother, who keeps reappearing."

While she had the floor, Marilyn asked about making the phone call. "I'd like to contact the doctor at the mental hospital from where Underwood escaped. His physician would be our best source of behavioral information."

The captain didn't hesitate. "Permission granted, Doctor Monrose. And thank you for the clues to his identity you've already provided. We have not found any of the killer's DNA at the scene of the murders. We have Underwood's on file though, so if he gets sloppy, we can try for a match. Since our suspect is a fugitive, I'll work on getting clearance to start circulating his photo."

"If he sees his picture, he might dig in deeper or take flight," Hudson pointed out.

"A chance we'll have to take. We need to list him as a person of interest, the women out there deserve a heads up. Surveillance will be posted at the train and bus stations, the airport, and rest stops and gas station on the major highways.

"We believe he would be living on limited funds, which will in turn limit his mobility. This is a think-tank operation, so whatever anybody comes up with, no matter how trivial or seemingly unimportant, feed the information back to central."

The captain stood, indicating the meeting was at an end. Amongst muttered theories and comments, the room cleared.

"Doctor Monrose, why don't you use my office to

call Underwood's physician. I'd like to be present when you do so."

Marilyn appreciated his tact. She knew the department's trust in her was limited. "Yes, of course. I'm ready if you are."

Hudson insisted on being present too, and once situated in the office with the door closed, she placed the call and switched to speakerphone.

"Hello. Yes, I'm trying to reach Dr. Bursak please."

"This is Dr. Bursak. How may I help you?"

"This is Dr. Monrose. I'm working with the Denver Police Department in an effort to locate your missing patient, Archibald Underwood. Might you answer a question or two for us?" The following pause seemed eternal. "Dr. Bursak?"

"Yes, yes, I'm still here. I worked personally with Archie for many years, and his escape has stricken me to the core. You already have a plethora of medical information which I was forced to release. I'm reluctant discussing his case any further. Patient confidentiality and all."

"I can appreciate your position and the protective feelings you might have for Mr. Underwood. But we're concerned he might be involved locally in a spate of criminal activity."

"Do you have proof he's committed any crimes?"

She scribbled on a scratch pad and held the question up to the captain. When he nodded his consent, she continued.

"I'm about to share with you evidence which has not been released to the press or the general public, and the details need to stay that way. No one beside the men and women working on the case are aware of this information. Do you understand?"

"Yes, I understand. Please go on."

"As you probably know, Denver has recently experienced a series of murders. The victims are females of various ages, all employed in occupations requiring them to wear a white lab coat type uniform. What hasn't been released to the public is the fact each victim has had her right hand cut off and taken from the scene."

They heard a strangled pain-filled sound. "What do you want to know?" Dr. Bursak's tone shifted from confrontational to defeated.

"Since Mr. Underwood is no longer on any of his medications, we are concerned he may have reverted back to his original psychotic mental state. Knowing what compulsive or unusual behavior he exhibited could help us in locating him. Did he have any hobbies or fixations?"

"Cats. He loved cats—was fanatical about them. Big cats especially. He talked about them, read about them, studied them. You would be amazed by the facts he could tell you about the feline species. He is quite the authority on them.

"There were times he even considered himself a cat. During those spells, he refused to eat anything but raw meat. He declared cats should rule the world, hunting and killing those who were evil. We finally gave him a pet cat, to which he grew overly attached."

"How did he treat the live animal?"

"He adored it. Unfortunately, the cat eventually passed away leaving him inconsolable. In retrospect, giving him a pet hadn't been the best of ideas. The animal's death set him back years as far as his mental improvement. The cat's demise reminded him of the death of his childhood cat. The one his mother strangled right before his eyes. We gave him a stuffed tiger and, in due course, he fed and cared for the toy as if it were alive."

"So, an affinity for cats featured largely in his mental makeup and his mental breakdown. Did he have a tattoo?" Marilyn was sure what the answer would be.

"Yes. A small one above his ear, on the side of his head, Cat Man. He did it to himself by grinding up pencil lead, mixing the dust with water, and puncturing the slurry into his skin with a safety pin. He usually wore a knit cap, so we didn't realize what he was up to until the area got infected and needed treatment. By then the deed was done."

Her gaze met Hudson's. He gave her the thumbs up sign for knowing about the tattoo.

"Anything else, Dr. Bursak? Anything at all that might help us to locate him?"

"Not really. On rare interludes, he seemed as normal as you or I. But his mind is fractured—how else could he live with what he'd done as a young boy? He wasn't allowed to attend his mother's funeral. And he was terribly upset when we took her severed hand from him. I believe in his mind she still lives and controls him."

Marilyn drew a big question mark on the paper and flashed it to Hudson and the captain. They both shook their heads no, indicating they didn't have anything they wished to add or have her mention.

"Thank you, Dr. Bursak. I appreciate your time. Please call back at this number if anything helpful comes to mind."

"He likes to be called Archie." There was sadness in Dr. Bursak's voice as if he knew this was not going to end well.

The line went dead.

"Come on. I have an idea." Hudson gained his feet and hurried from the office, Marilyn and Captain Bradshaw on his heels. "Marco, do you still have the map we used when we busted up that drug cartel near City Park?"

"Yeah, it's in here." Marco dug through a metal cabinet containing station house odds and ends. As he freed the rolled-up map, Hudson cleared off one end of the nearest desk. Far from new, and tattered at the corners, the detailed street map included topography. "What are we looking for?"

"When we were on stakeout there at night, we occasionally heard the big cats at the zoo roaring and scuffling about. Maybe our guy is hanging out near there."

Marilyn nodded in agreement. "Of course. His obsession with cats would be the perfect draw. The Denver Zoo is pretty famous, and he definitely could have read about the tigers kept there."

Marco tapped a finger on the map. "He'd be within walking distance of fast food. And with camps of the homeless and junkies nearby, one more person living rough would blend in no sweat."

"Construction is going on in the area too," Hudson put in. "Old houses being torn down to make room for more high-rises. Any one of several abandoned locations could work as his place of shelter."

"All of the murders were relatively close to the

area." They all turned to look at the map beside the white board—red pins marked the location of each of the victims' last moments on Earth.

"Start a grid search of the area," the captain ordered. "Concentrate on the area surrounding the zoo. I have a special request for the two of you." He nodded at Marilyn and Hudson. "After which you are to lay low for a while."

Hudson came to attention—defiance etched on his face. "Why would we do that?

"Apparently Dr. Monrose is the soup of the day. By now I'm sure there are reporters waiting outside the station, front and back. Since you can't leave undetected this time, you can draw them off, so they won't follow my men. Then you can stay put at your homestead."

Marilyn didn't miss the emphasis on the words *my men*. Although she guessed he probably wouldn't have changed things, she knew Hudson missed being one of the boys. Independence had its price.

"Take it or leave it. And by leave it, I mean you're both out altogether."

An expression of frustration froze on Hudson's face, and she could only imagine the words and phrases careening through his mind behind the stillness. He unclenched his jaw but evidently bent his mind to the logic. "If that's how we can help, then all right. But keep us posted. I can't promise to stay away for long."

As Marilyn and Hudson turned to leave, Marco answered a call on his cell phone. Before they could reach the squad room's door, he waved them back. "Hey, Hud, wait a minute. They found Warren Jameson's rental car."

Anxious to learn more, they waited for Marco to finish his phone conversation. “Are you sure? I’ll send out forensics and be right behind them.” Marco hung up. His hesitation to speak guaranteed bad news.

Marilyn’s shoulders slumped. “He’s dead, isn’t he?” Warren had been a mercenary, a conceited jerk, and in the end a traitor to all she held dear. But dead? Quite the extreme payback for his bad decisions and gambling addiction. She’d hung around with Warren. His death brought the horror close to home.

“Any details on what happened?” Hudson threw out the question she couldn’t find her voice to ask.

“It’s all speculation until the crime scene unit and the coroner are done with him.”

“Then how about where did they find him, and you must have at least an estimate on time of death.”

Had Warren’s body been discovered soon enough for her to run her VR program on him? Could she withstand seeing his death? The process was hard enough on a stranger.

“The car is out on I-70 in a turnoff between Floyd Hill and Idaho Springs.” Marco referred to the map on the white board. “It’s been there at least three days.”

Three days. What a relief. Fate had taken the problem out of her hands.

Hudson touched her arm. “He must have died the night he came to your house, Marilyn. He can’t be the person who set your place on fire.”

She hadn’t considered the timeline in that respect. Warren being responsible would have neatly tied things up on her arson case. This realization left room for questions and concern regarding the incident.

“Sorry it wasn’t better news. I gotta run.” Marco

pocketed his iPhone.

"Thanks, buddy. Talk to you later." Hudson leaned back on the desk. "I'm sorry it wasn't better news too. I understand you and Warren were close at one time."

"Not as close as you might imagine, still his passing comes as a terrible shock and not without grief. Lately, I'm having trouble making heads or tails out of what is going on around me."

One thing she knew for sure, the Kingsley Institute would be in an uproar over Warren's death and over her making the news. The higher-ups and their benefactors liked cruising under the radar. Jade must not be aware of what had transpired, or she'd be calling.

The phone in her pocket sang out. Speak of the she-devil, a text from Jade. But not about Warren, about the newspaper photo and article. The big boss wanted to see her immediately. Would they go so far as to suspend her?

Her contract with Kingsley was nearly up. Never a fan of the way they kept tabs on their employees and their work, dictating parameters, pressuring people with unrealistic deadlines—she needn't renew, could cut the ties.

The VR project had been totally her idea. Finding the concept interesting, they allowed her to develop the theory on the side. But there were main projects they insisted she work on. How her part in these ventures fit into the whole was kept secret from her. Kingsley may not be doing anything wrong or illegal, but she didn't want to be involved in their covert game plan anymore.

"I need to check in at the lab. Will you take me?"

"Sure. We can stop there first and lead the news hounds a merry chase."

She shot a text back to Jade, alerting her boss she'd be there shortly, yet she failed to move. A whirlwind of serious decisions consumed her. She wasn't sure which way to turn or what might be a misstep rather than a smart move, altering her course forever.

"Are you ready?" Hudson prompted. "What are you thinking?"

She was thinking if she had another place to set up her lab, she could go solo. Which meant either rebuilding her scorched house or selling and starting over. Both prospects sounded exhausting, overwhelming.

"Marilyn?" He gently tugged at her shirtsleeve.

"What? Oh, yes, I'm coming." She needed to snap out of it and take care of the here and now. She had a feeling her future would depend on choices made today.

As she stowed her phone, he took her hand. "Come on, doctor, time to face the paparazzi."

Chapter Fifteen

She hadn't been suspended—they'd fired her ass. *Clean out your locker* was the only phrase they hadn't used.

Being called on the carpet because of the news article was bad enough, but by the time Marilyn reached the inner sanctum at Kingsley, Warren's death had come to light as well as her liaisons with him. That nosy Ruth Anne in geophysics must have spilled the beans.

They barely gave her time to grab her spare lab coat before escorting her to the Human Resources department to relinquish her badge and key card. All done under the guidance of a security guard. Thank heaven she'd proactively removed her personal equipment.

Head spinning with anger, hurt, and even a little self-pity, she stepped onto the elevator for the last time. When the doors opened, Hudson was waiting for her in the lobby.

Usually self-sufficient and full of bravado, she'd never needed anyone. But lately, she felt adrift in a leaky boat on an angry sea. And PI Kincaid seemed to have become her safe harbor, her port in the storm. The sight of him eased her pain.

"So, are your ears bleeding?"

She shook her head no.

"In the old days, I've worn that expression a time or two after a brutal dressing down from Captain Bradshaw."

"It's worse than a dressing down. I got sacked."

"Holy… Gees, talk about overreacting. What did they say?"

"I have to pay back my starting bonus, and they had me sign a nondisclosure agreement."

"Nondisclosure on what?"

"All my projects initiated by them. They agreed to terminate my contract early without a penalty, and they allowed to me to keep the rights to my VR project."

"Wow, I'm surprised.

"Me too." She felt she'd scored a victory there. "Kingsley never knew the bottom line on what I'd discovered. Because the ramifications were so far reaching, I kept a large part of it a secret. Anyway, the universe seems to be telling me to move on. Too bad I haven't a clue as to where that might be."

"I've got an idea."

"I can't keep living with you forever."

"Why not?" His tone indicated he wasn't joking. "Have you got a better offer?"

"No. But…oh I don't know."

"Your independent streak is showing. At least consider the idea."

"I promise I will. Now we had better go."

Heads down, they pushed through the double front doors of the building. In a repeat performance of the other day, the press came alive, surging toward them like a giant multiheaded beast. Using their previous tactic, they made a beeline for the truck. Remotely unlocking the doors, Hudson scrambled in behind the wheel and Marilyn jumped in the passenger side.

Like a band of roving zombies, hungry for brains, the news people clawed at the vehicle and pounded on the windows as Hudson whisked them out of the parking lot. The mob ran down the street behind them for nearly a block before giving up. Fortunately, the throng of news hounds doubled back to follow up the story now involving the Institute.

****

By the time they reached the turnoff to Hudson's place, Marilyn's anxiety and anger had lessened. Deciding she might as well enjoy her forced liberation, an unexpected sense of relief in both mind and body settled over her. Too late, she'd realized institutions like Kingsley and Big Pharma quietly ruled the planet. She was glad to be rid of them before she became more entangled and indebted to the machine.

When they reached the edge of Hudson's property and the truck rolled to a stop, she hopped out, opened the gate, and waited for him to drive through. Then she dragged the panel closed. The action felt nice and familiar like she'd done it a hundred times. When they arrived at the house, Frank and Joe Hearty bounded over, acting almost as happy to see her as Hudson. The country surroundings and the unique experience of being part of a farm-family was beginning to seep into her bones.

"Before we go in, I want to show you the greenhouse."

Tired and longing for nothing more than solitude, she reluctantly agreed. Her effort was rewarded when she spied the enchanting Victorian structure with the attached brick potting shed.

"There's plenty of room for your equipment here. Electricity and water are already available and in working order. And before winter sets in, I can install baseboard heat or free-standing heaters for you."

Before winter? She glanced at Hudson. He was picturing her being here months down the road. The concept was a whole lot of wonderful, and a good bit of frightening. Hanging on to that thought she followed along as he led her closer.

The ornate oak door had a rounded top, reminiscent of an old Irish cottage. The panel squeaked and squawked when forced open, and crossing the threshold felt like stepping into another dimension.

"Oh, Hudson, it's magical. Between daydreaming and wanting to curl up in here with a good book, I'm not sure how much work I'd get done."

Artful brickwork covered the floor, and walls of wrought iron and thick glass rose to meet the wood paneled ceiling. With the nooks and crannies layered in decades of dust, the structure seemed charming and full of ancient stories. She would love to work in this beautiful setting.

"As a child I spent hours in here. Back then, towering plants created a jungle to be explored. And when Aunt Betty allowed her parakeets to fly around in here, I pretended they were birds of the Amazon."

For Hudson to share such a personal memory touched her deeply. She pictured him as a little boy and bet he wore a cowboy hat then too.

Now only forgotten brittle plants spilled from the huge cement flowerpots, wistful memories of the past glory he talked about. "It will take quite a bit of work to bring it around. Are you sure you want to commit to fixing this up and to giving me an open-ended invite?"

He settled one arms across her shoulder and snugged her near. "I'm sure. It's been great having you around. As far as commitments, I'm not asking for anything serious, just that you give the greenhouse/lab and us a try. Heck, we've already been through a few intense experiences, and we've come out the other side intact. We make a good team."

In her heart she already knew her answer, but she let him ramble on.

"Besides, Frank and Joe Hearty think you're the greatest, and they don't like just anybody."

"Don't forget Jubilee and Jessabelle—they approve of my ponytail holders."

"My critters aren't the only ones who like you, Marilyn."

"I like you too, Hudson—I mean really. I don't want to mess up what we have, but if you're sure you want me to stay, I say yes. And a huge thank you for taking me in."

She slipped one arm around his waist, resting her head sideways on his shoulder. He held her tight, and a hug had never felt so good.

"I'm planning on selling my house in Denver." Whether she ended up here or not, that idea was a done deal. "I had high hopes for my place. But after the fire and what happened with Warren, it's not the same. But I'm not good with big changes."

Hudson eased her aside and turned to face her. "New beginnings can be tricky, and having you staying here will be new for me too. As far as us, we can take things as fast or as slow as you like."

The sincerity in his voice had Marilyn wanting him

all the more. She slipped her hands inside his jacket and tugged at the warm flannel fabric beneath. “I’m happy to inform you I’ve definitely moved past taking things slowly.” With a more concerted effort, the snap buttons down the front of his shirt popped open one by one.

“Halleluiah. I was barely hanging on myself.” He tightened his embrace—heated kisses followed.

She drew back. “Much as I’m beginning to appreciate the great outdoors, could we go inside?”

“Good thinking. We’ll save getting back to nature for another time—under the stars.”

He took her hand and led the way, and she got that giddy-as-a-schoolgirl feeling again—what a delight. In the past, she may have enjoyed primal urges without commitment, but now she anticipated making love—a totally new and exciting experience.

Hudson’s room had a rustic beam ceiling and one huge mother of a brass bed. But when he slid one hand beneath her hoodie and T-shirt, architectural details faded and blurred.

As evening fell, muting the light, they tore at one another’s clothing. Joyful laughter rang out between the murmurs of eagerness and groans of anticipation.

****

Archie kicked the homeless woman and stole the late edition newspaper from beneath her head. He hated the useless transients. They didn’t even try to do better, and they cut into his panhandling trade. Besides, they had hair—that really stoked his ire. Long hair, which they didn’t even bother to keep clean.

Stumbling down the incline back into the basement and the dark world he knew best, he lit a candle and skimmed through the paper. The doctor woman was in the news again, wearing her white coat. The article said her house had caught fire. They even gave the address.

As a new plan formed amongst the chaos in his mind, the buzzing in his brain receded just a bit. He smiled and nestled the tattered stuffed tiger against his cheek.

With few exceptions, cats who purred couldn’t roar, and cats who roared couldn’t purr.

He never purred.

Chapter Sixteen

Before opening his eyes to the new day, Hud took a moment to savor Marilyn's warmth as she lay beside him in bed.

They'd made love twice. The first time loud, fast, and hard—driven by their pent-up hankering for one another. The second time, slowly and carefully. Both times more amazing than he'd imagined.

Peeking sideways, his gaze met hers, and she asked what he was already thinking. "How is it what we did last night didn't kill one or both of us?"

"I have no idea." Shifting onto his side, he draped one leg across her thighs. "The question will definitely require more testing. I know how much you like double checking your findings."

"I'll block out time for you on my schedule." She turned to face him, and his leg slid up and over her hip. "Right now, I need food. I always seem to be starving out here."

"Probably the country air. In or out of bed, I love a lady with a good appetite."

She blushed at his insinuation. He gave her a peck on one rosy cheek. She murmured something he didn't catch and buried her face against his chest. Cuddling had not been part of his ex's repertoire. He enjoyed the warm peaceful contact…a lot.

A discordant heehawing and huffing shattered the

blissful moment, followed by a high-pitched whinny and several bleating yelps.

"Gees, it's almost noon. No wonder they're making such a row. I better go feed them before old Buck wanders over to see what all the ruckus is about."

Reluctantly untangling himself from Marilyn, Hud sat on the edge of the bed with his back to her. "I need to check the stock tank too," he informed her. "The water level was getting low, and with the wind last night, it's probably full of dust and debris this morning. Would you rustle up the leftovers while I'm out?"

"Of course." She raked the fingernails of one hand across his naked back.

His flesh tingled, and renewed desire shot through him. What he wouldn't give to lie back down for round three. Then the dogs started barking too. This was as bad as having a passel of kids. Marilyn gave him a shove off the bed. He was glad she seemed to take in stride the morning chaos and interruptions.

Stark naked, he wandered around the room trying to reclaim the clothes they'd ripped off one another in haste. When he straightened to shag into his boxers, he caught her watching and didn't miss the raised brow and her smile of appreciation.

She made quite the picture herself with her dark hair loose and haloed about her head and shoulders. Since spending time in the country, she used less makeup, and her cheeks were tan. She'd also traded in her expensive high heels and designer sneakers for a pair of cowgirl boots and a set of rugged lace-up hiking boots—both sat beside the bed. He was almost afraid of feeling so happy.

Gathering her clothing, he tossed them to her. Not

requesting he leave or exhibiting any shyness, she dropped the quilt and tugged the Henley top over her head. Then she slid from beneath the cover and, going commando, pulled on her jeans. As he crossed the room, he almost smacked into the dresser.

"Since I've decided to stay here, I'm going to need more clothes." She straightened the coverings on the bed, and sitting on the edge pulled on and tied up her clutter boots. "And I'd like to check on my house. Maybe the structural inspection is finished, and I can line up someone to start on the repairs. Those will have to be taken care of before I can list it for sale."

Standing, she rubbed her hands together. "I can pick up some essentials too—like cream rinse for my hair, and about a gallon of hand lotion. Farm living is sure tough on a gal's beauty routine."

By the tone of her voice, he knew she was kidding. She hadn't issued one complaint in all the time she'd spent here. "If you want, I can go with you. It gets dark earlier these days, and you might want to grab something requiring heavy lifting."

"Thank you. That would be great."

In the kitchen, she started shuffling pots and pans. "I hope the smoke from the fire didn't ruin the new Victoria Secret pretties I left behind. Still in the box, they're probably safe."

He hesitated on his way to the mudroom. "Victoria Secret?"

She nodded and struck a provocative pose.

His imagination took flight quicker than the sage grouse he scared up on the way to the barn.

****

Visualizing how she would model the skimpy

outfits, Marilyn was warming up quicker than the remnants of last night's supper. Making love to Hudson had been wildly fulfilling, yet she still wanted more. And being intimate hadn't seemed to hurt their relationship. If anything, this morning they were even more in sync.

Alongside the scrambled eggs, she seared a piece of the venison steak for him and tossed in some asparagus for herself. Odd fare for breakfast, but they both appeared to be fans of making the best of leftovers. Another area in which they thought alike.

They… Was she already picturing Hudson and her as a they, a couple, a what? Take a breath, she cautioned. Then a Marilynism popped into her head, warning her to stop being so analytical. *You have to take a chance. Falling in love has nothing to do with the laws of gravity. It's not science, there are no rules or formulas. That's why it's so wonderful. And a little bit scary.*

Her happy mood returned. "Thank you, Marilyn."

Taken by an urge to bake, no doubt New Brain information from Becky Chapman, she turned on the oven. While it warmed, she rummaged around the cupboards grabbing sugar, flour, salt, and baking soda. Raiding the fridge once more she grabbed butter and an egg.

There wasn't any milk. The vanilla flavored coffee creamer would have to serve as a substitute. She threw together a batch of scones, cut the dough into wedge shaped pieces, and popped them in to bake.

As she straightened and dusted the flour from her hands, the term wifely flashed through her mind. Yikes. She'd never before pictured herself as a married woman. She was strong and liberated and didn't need a man to make her way in the world. But having Hudson along for the journey felt good so far. To be cared for and worried over was intoxicating. Would this emotional libation leave her with a hangover of regrets?

Out of a job and ready to cede the house, she had better be sure she hadn't agreed to Hudson's offer because she was in dire straits and afraid of the future.

"Change of plans." Hudson came through the back door, took off his hat and coat, and hung them up on the wall pegs. Coming up behind her standing at the stove, he peered over her shoulder at the food. "Boy, the kitchen never smells this good when I'm cooking."

"What's going on? What happened?" She gave him a nudge with her backside, trying to turn his attention away from the food and onto what he'd seemed about tell her.

"The heehawing and carrying on out there was regarding more than a late breakfast." He paused a moment to wash his hands. "By the time I showed up, the horse and donkey had wandered onto old Buck's property."

She handed Hudson both plates of food which he placed on table.

"What happened, are they all right?" Retrieving the scones from the oven, she set them beside the plates and the butter and honey. They both sat down.

"Over by the ditch, the wind blew down a limb from the cottonwood tree. Crash-landing on the fence, there was enough damaged to allow Pepper Jack and Hank to sneak through to go visiting."

"Why didn't Buck come and get you?"

"He says he kept an eye on them, but he didn't

want to disturb me when I was entertaining my lady friend. Besides, he figured I'd eventually discover my horse and donkey had gone missing."

"Am I your lady friend?" she teased.

Hudson reached across the table and took her hand. "Yes, ma'am. My lady friend and my best gal. And I love you even more than that ornery horse that ran off." The extra bit of cowboy twang in his voice had her laughing. And although she knew he was kidding, hearing him say those words gave her heart a flutter.

"Old Buck seems remarkably up to date regarding what goes on over here."

"He's a good guy. Mostly, he's bored. A widower like Uncle Louie, out here he has limited social contacts. He's always ready to help a neighbor, but he also considers us his entertainment.

"Anyway, I need to take care of the fence. I don't use barbed wire, but an unsuspecting animal could get tangled and hurt in the broken section. The repairs could take a while. Which means not going into Denver right away. Or maybe not today at all."

"No problem. I can drive there on my own. I'll take my car."

His brow furrowed as he chewed a piece of venison. "It's already well into the afternoon. I wish you'd wait until I could go with you. Or wait until tomorrow."

"No way. I'm on a mission. My skin is like sandpaper. The udder cream you gave me helped, but designed for cows, I found the formula a bit lacking in aesthetics."

He held up his hands as if to ward off an attack. "Okay, you win. Obviously, there'll be no stopping you. At least promise to text me when you get to your house. Lately, no matter the time of day, I-25 is a nightmare of heavy traffic, DUI's, and accidents. And don't forget it gets dark—"

"Early these days. I know."

Chapter Seventeen

The fence repair had taken longer than Hud anticipated. Finally satisfied with his work, he sent the F-150 bouncing over the prairie back to the house—Frank and Joe Hearty on the truck seat beside him.

When his cell phone chirped, he hoped it was Marilyn. She'd texted him when she'd reached her home, but that was hours ago, and he hadn't heard from her since.

"Oh, hey, Marco. What's up?" His brief disappointment turned to concern as to why his friend would be trying to reach him.

"We ran algorithms on the locations of the murders and the area around the zoo where the big cats would be audible. Now we're doing a door to door based on those parameters. This guy would be a hard face to forget, but we haven't had any luck so far. With this new strategy, we could use another set of boots on the ground. Where are you now?"

"At the farm."

"Figures. I would be too if I had Dr. Monrose to curl up with in front of a nice warm hearth."

"It's a woodstove, and right now Marilyn's at her house. I'll leave her a message so she knows what's going on and where to find me. By the way where exactly will that be?"

"We set up a command post north of the Denver

Zoo on 27th, one block west of Colorado Boulevard. Murphy's Bar & Coffee Shop offered up the use of their backroom for a gathering place, free coffee even. When your shift ends though, you gotta pay for any drinks. But nobody's shift ends until we catch this creep."

"I'll be there as soon as I can."

****

Uber. He liked the sound of the weird new word. Uber, Uber, Uber.

The man at the gas station told him he could call for a car to come and pick him up and take him anywhere he desired to go. So many new possibilities.

As he waited with anticipation for the sun to set, a last ray of light burst though the broken pane of glass. The cracks angled the illumination upward across his trophies, casting giant shadows on the crumbling brick wall at his side. He drew back, startled by the unexpected and frightening image of distorted hands and clawing fingers.

Maybe he'd leave a little early tonight. Leaping to his feet, he grabbed the coveralls, his knife, and money for the payphone.

****

Driving to her house, Marilyn couldn't wait to grab the items on her list and lock the place up—metaphorically never looking back. But now she discovered walking away turned out to be harder than anticipated.

When you live at a place, even for three years, you make memories. And whether good or bad they were a part of you. There were expectations and dreams thrown into the mix also, which stirred up her sentimental side—a condition to which she rarely yielded. Hopefully new dreams awaited, ones including Hudson.

She glanced around the foyer. Her car was packed to the gills and ready to go, so there was no excuse for lingering. She'd emptied the fridge, and taken out the stinky trash, and turned down the heat—keeping the temperature high enough to prevent any pipes from freezing if they had a cold snap. It was time to go.

Ambling through the house one more time, she turned off the lights as she went. With each click of the switch, the gathering darkness outside became more apparent. She had better get a move on.

Circling around to the ruined library, she gazed sadly toward her beloved, smoke-tainted collection of books—several were rare, all were important to her. Tomorrow, she'd call the Colorado Art Restoration Company on West Colfax. Their website appeared promising. They could professionally pack up her treasure trove and give her an estimate on the work needing to be done.

Right now, she had better let Hudson know she was on the way back to his place. Retrieving her iPhone from the table by the door, she found and read his message. She knew where Murphy's was located, she'd meet him there instead.

Before she could text him, the backdoor to the kitchen squeaked open—the tiny sound stopping her dead in her tracks.

"Hudson?"

****

Heading down Colorado Boulevard, Hud neared the DPD task force rendezvous site. On a whim, he checked in with Marco. "Any new developments?"

"Major. I just got a call. They think they found where he's been hiding. I'm leaving Murphy's now. What's your ETA?"

"I'm right up the street, a block to the north."

"Watch for me."

Marco came peeling out of the bar/coffee shop parking lot and headed south, lights flashing but no sirens. Accelerating, Hud swung into line behind his ex-partner. They drove about five blocks, turned left down an alley, and then ground to a halt side by side. A DPD squad car was already there.

The abandoned building was one of several structures waiting in line to be torn down. Six stories high, all the windows were busted out, and one corner of the foundation was caved in. A nearby streetlight, miraculously surviving destruction, cast a weak unearthly glow over the area.

One officer waited in front of the tumbled down facade. His features held a stricken expression. The illumination of a flashlight ebbing back and forth inside indicated another officer investigated on the lower level.

"Nobody else comes in," Marco ordered the man standing guard.

"Yes, sir." The officer nodded.

Hud hunched over and followed Marco through the jagged opening and down the makeshift steps. The immediate area, strewn with construction debris, held signs of recent occupation.

Waiting for his eyes to adjust to the dimness, Hud held his position. After a minute he shifted his gaze from side to side. There seemed nothing remarkable about the walls. Then he glanced upward and stumbled back in disbelief. In the shadowy darkness, the string of hands attached to the overhead rope were barely visible, yet their effect was profound.

"Sweet Mother of Mercy."

"To put it mildly."

"All four of the missing hands."

"But he left room for more." Marco stepped closer to the street officer waiting off to the side. "McMasters, report."

Hud tore his gaze from the overhead spectacle to listen.

The young man swallowed hard and came to attention. His expression took on more animation and less shock and revulsion. "Officer Lockhart and I were assigned to search the nearby area. Two blocks from here we noticed the employees at McCluskie's Auto Repair and Paint Shop were wearing plastic coveralls the color of the scrap found at one of the murder scenes.

"The business checked out okay, and they informed us when the coveralls were no longer useable, they were tossed out back in the trash. There's a sample in the squad car. From there we kept a straight course and questioned the man who runs the local gas station. He identified our guy right off. We called in the information and began a door to door, fanning out from the point of last seen.

"Then Officer Lockhart and I found this place, and…" His words trailed off as he gazed upward. Now his face contorted as if in pain.

Marco placed a hand on the young cop's shoulder and turned him toward the exit. "Good work, McMasters. Get the emergency light out of the squad car and set the equipment up down here. When you reported in, I called for backup. More officers are on the way. When they arrive, tell them to secure a one block perimeter, keeping a low profile. Lockhart stays at the door. Nobody in or out unless I say so."

McMasters nodded and moved to follow orders.

"Leave the flashlight," Marco suggested. The officer handed off the light as he hurried past. Marco played the beam on the exit so the young man could find his way out. Then he skimmed the slash of brightness across the dirty mattress, the empty food containers, and the used candle stuck in the top of an empty wine bottle.

A book of matches lay on the makeshift table. Not wanting to add his fingerprints to the mix, Hud jammed his hands in his pockets, resisting the urge to grab the matches and light the candle. Besides, he wasn't ready to view the hands with more clarity. What a delicate and yet monstrous sight they created.

With the emergency equipment in place, a harsh white light flooded every corner of the dank basement. Turning to leave, the young officer accidentally disturbed the rope strung across the ceiling. The hands gently waved as if drawing Hud near—as if whispering, "See what he did to us. Find him."

Now he couldn't stop staring at the display of depravity. Relative to the order in which they were obtained, the muscle and flesh had cured and shrunk to different degrees on various hands. But all the fingernails, expertly painted like tiny masterpieces, were bright and joyfully colored. The genius side of Archie's insanity.

He switched his focus to the rickety table. A recent

copy of the Denver Post lay on top. A prominent article showed an archive photo of Marilyn in her white lab coat. She held an award she'd won a few years back. The caption read *Scientist who may hold key to finding serial killer is victim of arson.* A plastic fast-food knife was stabbed into the picture.

Hud tried Marilyn's cell number. No answer. He texted her and checked for any new messages she may have left. Nothing.

"Marco, over here. The fools reported her address in the arson information. He could be headed there."

"Looks like a terrible possibility. While he was setting up the light, McMasters mentioned the gas station owner had called Archie an *odd duck* because he needed instructions on how to use Uber."

"So, he may not be on foot."

"I'll relay the info to central. There's a mounted patrol in her area. Dispatch can send him over. I can't leave until forensics gets here."

"I know. But I can, and I am."

The engine in his truck revving, Hud made the quickest three-point turn in history. Then knocking over trash bins and various piles of junk, he blasted down the alleyway and into the street. Tires squealing and drawing words of anger and several hand gestures, he wove in and out of the street traffic as he sped toward Marilyn's house.

****

"Who's there?" Frozen in place, Marilyn was sure she'd heard a noise in the kitchen.

"You are one hard bitch to kill."

Phone in hand, she turned toward the voice as a figure stepped out of the shadow.

"Who are you? Get out of my house."

"Hand over the phone, if you please. Or even if you don't, please." The woman slid a snub-nosed revolver from the pocket of her fleecy white jacket.

Marilyn keyed in a text message to Hudson, but the intruder knocked the phone from her hand before she could hit send. "Listen, whoever you are. My boyfriend is on his way here, and he carries a gun too, bigger than yours." Would that scare the woman off?

"I doubt he's really on the way, and he's my boyfriend, not yours."

"Jennifer?"

"So, he's mentioned me." An arrogant smile slipped into place on the other woman's face.

"Don't flatter yourself. The press wasn't good." Marilyn remembered Jennifer was a reporter—and apparently a crazy stalker. "You set the house on fire, didn't you?"

"Good guess. The loose board on the step seemed to be taking forever to bring you down, so I had to get more creative."

How many times had this horrible woman been inside her house? The idea sent a shiver down her spine. "If you're so in love with Hudson, why kill him?"

"I didn't realize he was in the house that night. He'd finally traded in his stupid old truck for a stupid new one, and I didn't recognize the vehicle parked out front as being his. Boy I hated riding in that old piece of junk. But I read his uncle died, and now Hudson owns that prime piece of real estate which he can sell for a mint, and we can buy a high-rise apartment and a Mercedes.

"But enough chitchat. Get moving." Jennifer waggled the business end of the nasty looking gun, indicating Marilyn should step farther back into the library.

She was getting tired of people waving guns in her face.

"No matter what you do to me," Marilyn challenged, "he's done with you."

"Well, you being a brainy scientist and all, I guess you'll understand if we put your theory to the test before the final analysis. Get over there where the boards are scorched."

Marilyn stared at the weakened floor. The unsafe for habitation sign was still tacked to the front door.

"I said get moving." Jennifer stamped her foot, and her eyes narrowed to angry slits.

What a choice. Get shot or fall down into the basement. Crashing through the hardwoods sounded pretty painful, but a bullet would be fatal.

"Where are the stairs to the lower level?" Jennifer glanced around.

"Why?"

"I doubt the drop will kill you. Post-fall injuries may be required to finish the job. But your death will still be listed as an accident."

"You're as crazy as the serial killer."

"I certainly am not. How insulting. That nutcase is a frigging psychopath. I'm simply trying to get back what's mine. I deserve Hudson. I stayed at the wretched farm with his uncle and those smelly animals for months. Now he's got money, and his PI business is getting big press from his working with the police on a prominent case. We should be together again."

As Marilyn wracked her brain for a way out of her desperate situation, she thought she heard a horse snorting in the front yard. She cocked her head toward the library window. The shades were drawn and the window closed, but the glass had cracked from the heat of the fire allowing sound to easily penetrate. There it went again—noises like Pepper Jack made at Hudson's place.

"Dr. Monrose. This is Officer Kendal, Denver Mounted Police. I'm at your front door which is locked. If you can hear me, will you please respond and open the door? I've been asked to check on your whereabouts and safety. Dr. Monrose, can you hear me, are you there?"

"Not a word," Jennifer whispered, training the muzzle of the pistol at the center of Marilyn's chest.

"Hey. You there. What the…?" The officer's voice trailed off and a scuffling sounded on the porch—followed by a heavy thud.

When Jennifer turned in surprise, Marilyn pounced. The gun flew from the other woman's hand as the two of them tumbled to the floor. Gaining her feet first, Marilyn kicked the other woman in the ribs—several times as hard as she could. Wearing her new hiking boots, the action had the desired effect, she heard bones cracking and felt no regret.

"Officer, help. I'm here inside." Marilyn glanced around for the weapon—or for an object with which to either hit or tie up Jennifer.

Holding her side, the reporter crawled toward the backdoor. The gun had skidded to a stop in the middle of the weakest floorboards. Abandoning the idea of retrieving the weapon, Marilyn hurried to the foyer.

Why hadn't the police officer replied to her calls for help?

She wrenched open the front door and nearly tripped over the man's inert form. Blood oozed from a wound on his head. Even more blood trickled from his thigh where a tear in his pant leg revealed a deep slash to the flesh. His horse stood dutifully nearby, shifting from one foot to the other as he nosed the downed officer.

"Nice horse. Easy now." Fearing the animal might interpret her actions as harmful rather than helpful, Marilyn approached cautiously and then squatted down beside the man.

Earlier, while gathering her clothes, she'd come across a red paisley scarf. Sliding the bandana from her neck, she tied the cloth around the officer's leg to lessen the bleeding. Although she never dressed western, the little scrap of material had always reminded her she lived in cowboy country. Her poor neckerchief, now completely red with blood, became a tourniquet rather than a jaunty tieback for her hair.

The bleeding slowed, but the officer was still out cold. Probably from the blow to his head. At least his breathing was regular, and when she'd checked at his wrist and neck, his pulse felt strong.

Warily, she glanced around and gained her feet. Who had attacked the officer? Had Jennifer brought an accomplice? Racing back inside, she scooped her cell phone up off the floor and dialed 911, requesting an ambulance for the injured policeman.

Checking for messages, she noted Hudson had tried to reach her. Distracted by the chaos, she hadn't heard the incoming alert. She returned his text and hurried to the kitchen and out into the backyard. She wasn't about to let Jennifer get away. The woman seemed the persistent type, and Marilyn didn't intend to always be looking over her shoulder, worrying when the crazy woman might strike next.

"Help me, somebody, help me please." Jennifer was screaming at the top of her lungs.

Marilyn slipped the phone into her pocket and peered through the darkness. The other woman's stark white windbreaker stood out like a ghostly vision, everything else seemed lost to the shadows.

"Make him stop," Jennifer shrieked, kicking out and rolling from side to side.

Was it a trap to lure her into the yard? Heart pounding, Marilyn squinted trying to discern what was happening? Grabbing a garden rake, she eased forward. As her eyes adjusted, she made out an altercation near the fence line.

Jennifer was on the ground, a dark figure hovered over her. Marilyn plowed through a pile of dry autumn leaves, they crunched beneath her feet, and the person hurting Jennifer hesitated and jerked upright. Then he turned in her direction.

He wore a cap covering his hair, or lack thereof, but she knew those eyes. She'd stared into them three times before, and each time the cruel madness emanating from them said someone was going to die.

"Not this time, Archie," Marilyn yelled, drawing his full attention.

Confusion showed in those eyes, and he glanced back and forth between her to Jennifer. "You're the wrong one," he accused, snarling down at the woman on the ground.

With a whimper, Jennifer curled into a ball, covering her head with her arms as if this might protect her from the knife Underwood wielded.

"It was supposed to be you." He straightened and faced Marilyn full on.

"It wasn't supposed to be me or any of them. I'm not your mother. They were not your mother. She's gone. You must stop this now."

She thrust the rake like a jousting lance. Archibald Underwood stood his ground and roared, and she retreated a few steps. The distant wailing of an ambulance siren broke through her fear, and the eerie sound gave her hope.

Archie recognized the sirens too. With his free hand, he snatched off his hat and threw it to the ground. "You tricked me." He screamed out the words with such visceral hate, they hung in the cold night air like solid objects.

As if tearing out hair that didn't exist, he pawed at his head. Then Archie's demeanor suddenly changed as if he'd been slapped across the face. He came to attention facing Marilyn, and his calmness was nearly as frightening as his hysterics.

Archie took a step forward.

Marilyn took step back.

Since he'd stopped ranting, maybe she could get through to him. "My name is Marilyn. I'm a doctor, won't you let me help you?"

"Doctors don't help. They couldn't stop mother from coming back. No one can."

"Your mother isn't here. Why don't you put down the knife?"

He advanced again as if she hadn't spoken.

Marilyn threw the rake like a javelin, hitting Archie in the chest and throat. He floundered backward, choking and coughing. But rather than going down, he regained his balance and stumbled forward.

Turning, she ran toward the side of the house. She could hear Archie following behind her. Her only hope was to make it to the street.

****

Skidding his truck to a stop on the front lawn of Marilyn's house, Hud jumped out before the vehicle quit rocking.

An ambulance had already arrived. Two first responders were attending an injured person on the porch. Please, God. Don't let it be her. He gritted his teeth in preparation for what he was about to see, then huffed out a big breath of relief. The victim was a male police officer.

"Can somebody do something about this horse?"

The injured man must be the mounted patrol Marco mentioned, and his horse appeared ready to panic. "Have you seen the woman who lives here?" Hud reached for the reins.

"No. Just this guy." Not glancing up, the EMT continued working to stanch the blood flowing from the officer's leg wound.

Hud led the horse out of the way, but before he could secure the animal, Marilyn materialized out of the dark nearly colliding with him.

"He's right behind me. He's got a knife."

Shifting Marilyn behind his back, Hud took the blow intended for her. The blade slashed deep across his chest. Although not a stab wound, the pain sent him reeling. He staggered, needing a moment to get his bearings.

Archie kept running across the street and over to Cheeseman Park.

The task force personnel had yet to arrive. Hud was on his own.

Fighting against the pain, he gentled the horse and then crawled up into the saddle. The reins nearly slipped through his bloody fingers as he sent the police horse into action.

The man he chased disappeared into the trees. Hud urged the horse to follow, and they crashed through the underbrush. With no moonlight for illumination, the going was difficult. Yet without hesitation the horse plowed through the fir tree branches, charging onward as if he knew the perpetrator they chased had injured his partner.

With his free hand, Hud wadded up the front of his shirt, pressing the material against the bleeding chest wound. Nothing like having the world's largest paper cut across your entire body.

Swerving hard to avoid a park bench, horse and rider broke free of the trees and into a small clearing. Way up ahead, Archie zigzagged across the meadow waving his knife, his incoherent words filling the air and trailing in his wake.

Before Hud could reach him, Archie gained access to the street running parallel to the park. He stepped into the lane of traffic. A vehicle skidded to a stop, missing him by inches. Before the driver could react, Underwood yanked open the passenger side door and climbed in.

The traffic was light, and the car took off making good progress up Race Street and then over to

Josephine. Well-trained, the mount Hud rode never faltered, and when Hud drew close enough to see through the window of the car, he made out Archie holding his knife to the terrified driver's throat.

They were circling around the much larger Denver City Park. The zoo. Archie was going to the zoo. Releasing the fistful of shirt, his fingers sticky with blood, Hud snagged his phone and alerted Marco to the probable destination. Cutting across the open space, Hud prayed he could get there first.

Although not yet October 31st, tonight the Zoological Garden would be packed with visitors for the traditional Halloween gathering called Boo at the Zoo and Boo After Dark. At the entrance, Hud's bloodied appearance and unexpected arrival on a horse was greeted by shouts of excitement rather than alarm. Mistaking him for part of the spooky event, the visitors swarmed closer, laughing and surrounding him.

The chaos grew louder as the car Archie had commandeered bounced over the cement parking barriers and skidded right in through the open front zoo gates.

When the vehicle lurched to a stop, the driver opened his door and flung himself to the ground, crawling and stumbling away. Archie leaped out from the other side and ran.

Trying not to injure any bystanders, Hud slid from the prancing horse and handed the reins to a fellow wearing a cowboy hat. As he chased their suspect on foot, he heard sirens growing louder. Marco was on the way.

The Edge, an overhead walkway for the tigers, appeared to be Archie's destination. Struggling to catch his breath, Hud felt woozy. He must have lost more blood than he knew. But Archie was almost within his grasp, and he wasn't about to let him get away.

The big cats prowled about, calling to one another as if they felt the confusion and danger in the air. Crossing the first safety barrier and howling back at the animals, Archie grabbed hold of the towering wall of chain link and rattled the fence back and forth.

"Give it up, Underwood. There's nowhere to run."

Paying no attention to Hud's words, Archie sought the scaffolding erected for the Halloween decorations. Scrambling upward past the second safety barrier, he lunged sideways and latched onto the next level of chain link fencing. Finding purchase, he shinnied sideways to the main support, then leaping from one metal beam to another, he made his way to the top of the enclosure.

Agitated by the disturbance, the tigers snarled and clamored about. The louder they roared—the more Archie laughed.

Hud tried contacting Marco. "Where are you, man?"

"We're at the entrance. Hang on, I have you in sight."

Archie stood erect on top of the catwalk—his arms outstretched. If he fell, there would be no saving him, which was okay with Hud if that's what it took to stop the killings.

Shaking his fists at the sky, Archie railed against whatever demons lived in his brain. "Look at them, Princess. Aren't they magnificent?" He pointed to the sleek felines gathered down below in the cage. "We're just like them. We rule the night." Dancing across the top he flirted with danger. He spun around, clapping his hands in glee. Then he tripped and with a startled expression, pitched over the edge hitting the ground with a sickening thud.

Hud staggered over to the crumpled body.

The madman who had caused so many deaths, lay face up, his expression remarkably innocent. A toy tiger slid from the breast pocket of his plastic coveralls, and as the light faded from Archibald Underwood's eyes, the word "Princess" floated into the night on his last breath.

Hud checked for a carotid pulse, making sure the monster was dead.

With a sob of relief, he slid to his knees and offered a prayer of thanks.

"Holy crap, Hud. You're bleeding bad." Marco helped Hud off to one side.

"Is Marilyn safe?" he asked between fits of pain. "How is the mounted patrolman?"

"Marilyn's right here. And when we left her house, the police officer was on the way to the hospital, sirens blasting. They don't run the lights and noise if the guy is beyond help."

Hud heard Marilyn calling his name. She dropped to ground at his side, shed the sweater she wore, and covered the wound on his chest.

Marco opened the squad car first aid kit he carried and placed it at her side. "I'll call for a third ambulance."

Keeping pressure on his chest with one hand, Marilyn used the other to snag the big sterile dressing on top of the supplies.

"Why a third ambulance? Who's in the second

one? Are you hurt? No, you're right here. I can't think straight."

Using her teeth Marilyn tore the paper covering off the bandage, then she made a quick swap between her bloody sweater and the fresh covering. "Jennifer your ex showed up at my house."

"Jennifer? Was she following a story?"

"More a case of becoming the lead in her own drama."

Still running on adrenaline, Hud struggled to sit up. Marco shrugged out of and then folded up his jacket. Placing the bundle beneath Hud's head he pushed him back down. "Take it easy, buddy. Everybody's okay."

"But what happened? I need to know."

Marilyn stroked his arm, and the effect settled him down as she enlightened him. "Jennifer was obsessed with getting you back. She's the one who loosened the floorboard on the stairs and set my house on fire. Tonight, she personally wanted to make sure I was out of the way for good, but the mounted patrol officer interrupted her. Then Archie showed up and attacked her."

"But Underwood had a newspaper picture of you in your white coat. We thought you were the target, right?" He aimed the question at Marco.

"Correct, and she was," Marco confirmed. "But Jennifer showed up wearing white too. When she left through the backdoor, Underwood mistook her for Marilyn."

"He went after Jennifer before I could stop him. I'm not sure why she thought you and I were a couple. Or why she even imagined you liked me. Maybe she saw us in your truck leaving Kingsley."

Fighting through the bleariness, Hud came up with a theory. "Or maybe she was the one who broke into my place looking for a story because I was working on the serial killer case. She would have seen all my information, including a notation on your file indicating I thought you were hot."

Marilyn tried not to laugh. "How sweet."

"And that's why Frank and Joe Hearty were locked in the barn, and they were tired because they'd been drugged. Jennifer was always on one kind of pill or another, she probably slipped them something to keep them quiet while she broke in."

"That makes as much sense as anything tonight. Now lie still." She smoothed his hair back from his brow. "What's taking so long?" She glanced up at Hudson's ex-partner.

"They're on the way," Marco reassured. "Time seems slow when a person you care a great deal for appears ready to give up the ghost."

"Do I look that bad?" Having trouble focusing, Hud's thoughts slid sideways.

"You are a bit pale." Marilyn put more pressure on the bandage.

"I've seen snowdrifts with more color," Marco razzed. "But we got him, Hud. Just like in the old days." Marco reached down and grasped Hud's hand in a show of solidarity.

The ambulance arrived, and Marilyn urged the first responders closer.

"If you boys can stop congratulating one another, we really need to get Hudson to the hospital—ASAP."

****

As they loaded up the man who had come to mean

so much to her in so short a time, Marilyn took a moment to gaze up at the sky.

Cold and clear, a blanket of stars canopied the night. LeAnn had died staring up at such a cosmic display. New Brain memories from each of the victims tumbled and flashed through her mind, almost as if she were flipping through a stack of photos. This time the visions were joyous and uplifting, and she knew they were saying goodbye.

"He can't hurt anyone else," she whispered, "rest in peace."

Epilogue

Four weeks later.

The weather was gloriously warm for November.

Marilyn gazed out the floor to ceiling windows in the greenhouse/lab. She had never been this content. Yes, content. A much-underrated word and condition.

Hudson had redesigned—and against her protests—paid to have the greenhouse remodeled. Awash in sunlight from morning to dusk, a towering bookshelf, a row of cupboards, and a long metal table occupied one side. And on the other, a small Victorian table and chair nestled together, creating a cozy nook perfect for reading or theorizing.

A string of bistro lights glammed up the outside, and inside updated fixtures ensured she could work into the wee small hours if she liked. But those days were over. She didn't intend to waste her evenings laboring away when such a special man awaited her in the house, or the barn, or like now out in this nature-stuff which she had come to cherish.

From her vantage point, she could see them all. Jessabelle and Jubilee, legally roaming free-range, nibbled on a pile of leaves blown up against the fence. Pepper Jack and Hank sought partial shade in the loafing shed, and Frank and Joe Hearty snoozed in a puddle of sun.

Eyes closed, Hudson reclined on a chaise lounge

beside the dogs. Having been in excellent shape and health prior to his injury, he had healed quickly. But suffering a substantial loss of blood, even after a transfusion there were times he still tired out easily—fortunately not when they were in one another's arms.

The mounted patrol officer made great strides too. As part of his rehab, he visited the farm a few days a week, talking cop shop with Hudson as they walked for miles around the pasture.

Who killed Warren remained a mystery. A mob hit related to gambling debts was the favorite hypothesis. Hudson promised to keep searching for more information.

Done for the day, Marilyn powered down her equipment, giving thanks for her magical workspace and for her new field of endeavor. Working on a new theory, and redesigning her machines, she discovered her research showed potential in the field of Alzheimer's and autism. No more death and sorrow. Hope and light were the watchwords from here on out.

Reaching for her jacket, she snuggled into the dark blue wool, taking care with her right shoulder which proved slow to heal. When she tackled Jennifer at her house that infamous night, she'd received her own set of nasty bumps and bruises.

Emotionally off kilter, the reporter had been indicted for arson with intent to do bodily harm, which meant jail time along with rehab for anger management and pyromania.

Marilyn dropped the attempted murder charge in trade for a lifetime stay-away order protecting both herself and Hudson. After all, if Jennifer hadn't shown up, Marilyn may have become Archie's fifth victim, or sixth counting his mother. The stab wound Jennifer received resulted in permanent lung damage—a pretty serious consequence for her actions. She sure had her headline story now.

Exiting the lab, Marilyn softly closed the door. How quickly she'd come to accept Hudson's place as *their place*, which was a good thing as she no longer owned her beloved Victorian money pit. After the repairs, and listed at a decent price, her house had sold quickly. And although difficult, the decision felt right. Nowadays, you'd have to drug and drag her to get her back to Denver.

Wearing her happy red cowgirl boots, she brushed through the tall dry grass and wandered over to sit near Hudson. At the rustle of her approach, he squinted open his eyes.

"Thank you again for all the changes you've made to accommodate my being here."

"You're welcome." He yawned with gusto and rubbed one hand across his face. "I could have done more today, if I'd been allowed to get any sleep last night."

Hudson had managed to rock her world into the wee small hours. She gave a girlish laugh—this particular New Brain phenomenon had lingered. "You're a good lover, but not a good patient. Night or day, you should be resting."

"You're a doctor," he countered. "You would have gotten me through any relapse."

"I'm a neuroscientist. I can only help you if you hit your head." Because her moniker included doctor, Hudson assumed she knew everything about any ailment he or the animals exhibited. Thank goodness for basic training—and the internet.

Jessabelle picked her way over to the colorful metal sign propped up against a large rock. As a surprise, Hudson had commissioned the work of art to go over the door of the greenhouse/lab. Delivered late this afternoon, they hadn't had time to hang the panel, but that was okay as this special present deserved a full-fledged ceremony, not a rush job.

Deciding the metal sign wasn't edible, the goat moseyed on, but Marilyn continued to study the colorful design and the words written in Spanish.

"How did you possibly come up with this idea?"

Hudson stretched his long, lanky body and grinned at her. "On a pain-ridden night, when you were still away packing up your house, I couldn't sleep and rifled through your precious Marilyn Monroe books. She had so much sadness in her life, yet she soldiered on with warrior-like determination. I can see why you admire her. Anyway, I read about the prophetic plaque she'd installed in the house where she passed away."

"*Cursum Perficio*," Marilyn quoted. "My journey is over."

"That's the one. But around here, Spanish seemed more fitting than Latin. Besides, I hope our journey is far from over."

"*La Aventura Comienza*," she sounded out the Spanish words.

"The Adventure Begins," he quoted in English.

"Oh, Hudson, I love it. I love you."

The words were out before she could stop them. Words she'd never said to any man. As she waited for a response, she clamped her lips together to keep from saying anything else she may regret.

Then Hudson said the words that could make or break a heart. “I love you too, Marilyn. I truly do.”

Her lips relaxed into a smile, and another phrase came to mind. *Once begun, may the adventure never end.*

A word about the author…

Gini Rifkin's books follow characters who are courageous and passionate about life, and when they meet sparks fly while danger often threatens. Her settings include the American West, Medieval and Victorian England, and contemporary fantasy. When not writing, Gini has the privilege of caring for her menagerie of rescue animals including ducks, geese, goats, rabbits, donkeys, and cats. Her writing keeps her hungry to learn new things, and she considers family and friends her most treasured of gifts. So, step back in time or into the future, where adventurous romance is waiting just for you.

https://ginirifkin.blogspot.com

Other books by Gini Rifkin…

Undercover Outlaw
Trapper's Moon
Cowboys, Cattle, and Cutthroats
A Cowboy's Fate
Special Delivery
Victorian Dream
Lady Gallant
Iron Heart
The Dragon and The Rose

~*~

Fae Warriors Series

Solace
Bliss
Portence

~*~

Australia Burns, Volume Two

Show Australia Some Love, book two. Waiting for Caleb

Thank you for purchasing
this publication of The Wild Rose Press, Inc.

For questions or more information
contact us at
info@thewildrosepress.com.

The Wild Rose Press, Inc.
www.thewildrosepress.com

CPSIA information can be obtained
at www.ICGtesting.com
Printed in the USA
LVHW011915220821
695822LV00008B/191

9 781509 237227